The
Shenandoah
Sharpshooter

Walt Ryan

Copyright © 2014 Walt Ryan
All rights reserved.

ISBN: 0990636615
ISBN-13: 978-0-9906366-1-8

This book is dedicated to the memory of all those that fought and died on both sides of the Civil War. May history not forget that they were individuals, each with a life, and loved ones, and a story of their own.

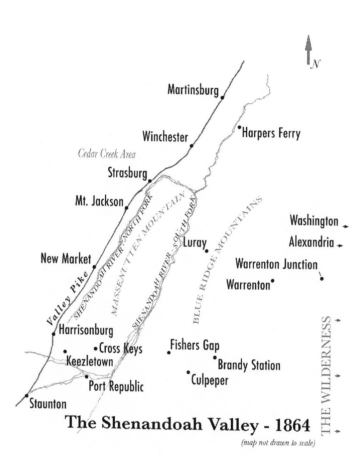

Martinsburg

Harpers Ferry

Winchester

Cedar Creek Area

Strasburg

Mt. Jackson

SHENANDOAH RIVER–NORTH FORK

MASSENUTTEN MOUNTAIN

SHENANDOAH RIVER–SOUTH FORK

BLUE RIDGE MOUNTAINS

Washington

Alexandria

New Market

Valley Pike

Luray

Warrenton Junction

Warrenton

Harrisonburg

Cross Keys

Fishers Gap

Keezletown

Brandy Station

Culpeper

Port Republic

Staunton

THE WILDERNESS

The Shenandoah Valley - 1864

(map not drawn to scale)

N

Chapter 1

Granville Coldiron stood up and brushed the dirt from the knees of his pants. His eyes searched up and then down the valley below. His gray shaggy head moved slowly on his hunched shoulders. Suddenly, he locked in on something in the distance. He squinted at the valley road for a few seconds, shielding his eyes against the mid-morning sun with his hand. "Don't stand up," he said to his younger companion kneeling over the potato row. "There are riders coming up the road. Where's Colonel Ben?"

"He's tied in the sprouts below the back stone fence. He still has the harness on," Stephen Purcell answered. "Who are they?"

Ignoring the question, the old man gazed intently down the valley road. He was uneasy. The younger man could tell.

Finally he answered, "They are some of Mosby's Loudoun County cutthroats, coming back here again. Somebody has told them they missed some stock. I can see at least a dozen of them. Listen close, boy. They'll be out of sight for a few minutes. When I give the sign, run to Ben, and take him up the hollow where the stock is hidden. Take the sack with the rest of the seed potatoes with you. Don't leave any tracks."

"Should I come back?"

"Stay there. Take the harness off Ben, and get ready to run. If they get too close, ride out. Go up into the mountains, you can lose them there. You can circle around, and come back in after a day or two.

"Now Stephen, they may go on without any problem, but if something happens to Eppie and me, you light out. You go west to get away from them. Don't come back until this damn war is over. Go on across the Alleghenies. Go into West Virginia, or better yet to Pennsylvania. Follow the same route we used to take the mules to Ohio. As long as you're on that horse you're safe. He'll outrun anything they got. Take care of him, and he'll take care of you.

"This place is your home. We have done signed it over to you. Bos Hartley and Mose both know about it. The banker has the papers. Now you take good care of Eppie's spring garden. Her garden has tolerable value. You can come back when all this is over."

The old man turned and looked at the youngster. "Remember what I've told you, boy. All right they're out of sight, get going." As an afterthought the old man said, "Don't go onto Massanutten Mountain unless you must. They could trap you against the river or the pike if they was a mind to." Then he turned and started down towards the house.

Stephen Purcell ran to the sack, snatching it and his buckskin jacket as he went by. Reaching Colonel Ben, he threw the potato sack and jacket across the big chestnut horse's withers. Jerking the picket rope loose, he grasped a harness hame and threw himself up behind the potatoes. Picking a path over hard ground, he traveled up the draw just below the crown of the hill and out of sight of the road.

The stock pen was under a large rock overhang. It was well-hidden and almost out of sight. The horse, a cow, and two sows had been kept there since the last raid on the farmstead the previous fall. Water trickled through the pens from a spring. Grain for the hogs was carried to the cave in sacks on Colonel Ben's back. The cow and Ben had been grazed in secluded fields, well away from the farmstead.

Purcell circled around hurriedly and came in from the far side, still trying to hide his tracks. He jumped down and pulled the harness and collar off the horse. He tied the rope to an oak sapling and raced back down the draw. He feared for the old man. Uncle Granville had said, "If something happens to Eppie and me..." Purcell figured Granville was expecting trouble. He disobeyed the order to stay put, without a second thought. His mouth was dry, his chest tight. He wasn't even conscious of his feet hitting the ground.

Purcell reached the lower stone fence and hurled himself over it. He paused to catch his breath. He heard shouting, followed by the crack of the squirrel rifle, and the thundering boom of a heavy caliber gun. There was more shouting accompanied by three pistol shots. Someone swore loudly. Then silence. Purcell crept along the fence on his knees. As he reached a vantage point over the yard below, he cautiously peered over. The scene below made him sick.

Eppie lay face down in front of the doorstep, the squirrel rifle still clutched in her hands. Granville lay motionless on the ground. A dead man in a Confederate uniform was sprawled a few feet behind his uncle, back against the wood pile, with his unsheathed saber lying across his legs.

Several feet away some of the raiders were standing over the body of another Confederate cavalryman. The woodpile axe lay nearby.

Purcell knew what had happened. The man with the saber had threatened or stabbed Granville. Eppie had grabbed the squirrel rifle and killed him. The other one had shot Eppie. Granville, in a fit of rage, killed Eppie's shooter with the axe. The raider mounted on the gray horse had shot Granville. The pistol was still in the raider's hand. He had deliberately put three balls into the old man.

Purcell dropped to the ground. He felt rage and despair. He was helpless, he could do nothing. He had no weapon except the old Green River butcher knife he had been using to cut the potato seedlings. If he only had a gun…

Purcell knew what he would do. He would wait. Wait for his chance. After the first raid, Granville had hidden his heavy old Hawken plains rifle and Ben's good plantation saddle with some other things under the floor of the house. Purcell planned to retrieve the rifle and saddle after the Rebs left. He vowed that he would hunt down the man with the pistol.

He looked again. Some of the raiders were looting the house. Others were digging graves in the corner of the yard. He slumped down again, unable to watch them bury Eppie and Granville. He fought back tears of grief, and finally the tears came. He sat there for a long time collecting himself.

Suddenly he heard a crackling sound and the smell of smoke reached his nostrils. The raiders were burning the house! The feeling of utter despair filled his gut again. All Granville and Eppie's belongings, the Hawken, the saddle, any supplies and utensils would be gone.

After a time, he heard the sound of men mounting up. He looked again to observe which way they were going. The bearded leader on the gray horse was sending them out in different directions. They were not leaving. They were searching for him.

Fear welled up in his throat. He fought the urge to jump up and run. The old man's words came to him. "When you get in a tight spot, don't panic, keep your wits about you. Act only as fast, or take as much risk as you have to." Purcell would crawl back down the fence and save his strength for a last chance sprint to the horse.

He crawled fifty yards, and looked through a hole between stones in the fence. Two riders were making their way toward him. One stopped at the stone spring house. One rider poked the door open with the barrel of his carbine. The other rider kept on coming up the fence.

That rider stopped a few feet down the fence to wait. Purcell slipped the knife from the sheath, gathered his right leg under him, and flattened against the fence. His mind raced. No, that would not work. He put his knife back. His only chance was to wait them out.

They came nearer and stopped on the other side. The one with the gravely voice eased his horse over against the fence. He was directly across the fence from Purcell. Purcell could see a patch of horse hair through the hole between the stones. If the rider looked over the fence he would see him.

The other raider said, "They got a cow hid somewhere, there was butter and a crock of fresh milk in the spring house."

"Yeah," Gravel Voice answered. "Striker said he'd been told they had some stock hid out as well as a hell of a good horse. The horse is a big Kentucky Saddler. He wants the horse. Striker is still a huntin' money, too. He says there is a boy here in his late teens. He wants to make the kid tell him if there is any money around. He says after we git the information, we need to kill the kid 'cause he knows we killed the old folks."

"I'll tell you what I think of that. Striker can do his own killing. I've had enough of shooting helpless old ladies and old men. I ain't for hurting no youngster."

"Yeah, me too," Gravel Voice responded. "That old man wasn't exactly helpless, though. One on one, I would have bet on the old man. Against any of us. Did you see the way he threw that axe? He just sort of scooped it up and brought it over his shoulder. It just sort of slipped out of his hands, right through the air. Bennington never knew what hit him."

"They say the old man was was a mountain man from the west," the other rider explained. "Bennington shouldn't have shot the old lady. She'd done all the damage she could do."

Gravel Voice gestured toward the disturbed earth farther up the hill. "They were using that horse to scratch up this potato patch. See that double shovel. The dirt on it ain't all dry, yet. The kid's hidin' out. I wish him luck. I hope him and his horse git away. A Kentucky Saddler is too damn good of a horse for the likes of Striker to be ridin', anyhow. We better be movin' on, or he'll be hollering at us."

Purcell waited until they were well away from him. Then he worked on down the rock fence. At the end, he snaked over the wall and crawled into the underbrush, retracing his earlier route.

When Purcell reached the overhang he went to the pig pen. He opened the panel gate. The hogs would survive if the raiders didn't find them. He let the cow loose. Grass was coming on and the cow was heavy with calf. The milk flow was about ready to dry up, anyhow.

Looking at the small sack of seed potatoes, he realized that he had some scant provisions after all. He tied the open end of the gunny sack securely with twine, then he distributed the potatoes evenly in both ends of the sack. Picking it up in the middle he placed the sack over the horse's shoulders. He pulled his jacket on to cover his easily-seen red shirt.

He picked up the harness bridle and despaired again at his lack of equipment. With the knife he cut the blinders off the bridle. Before this was over Ben would need to see on all sides.

He cautiously worked his way up the ridge. He turned the horse toward the top, knowing that he would probably be seen when he went over. There were four or five hours of daylight left. Once into the Blue Ridge he could lose them. When night came he would slip back, swim the river if needed, cross the Pike below Harrisonburg, and go into the Alleghenies. In his mind it was as simple as that. He would get supplies and equipment along the way, somehow.

There was a shout, followed by more shouts from below. They had found him. Purcell started over the crest, then he turned the horse around to face the riders below. He cupped his hands around his mouth to make his voice carry. "Come on, you women-shooting sons-of-Satan! I'll give you a run for your money!" His challenge was met with curses and a volley of gunfire. Over the crest he let the big horse pick his way down the timbered hill.

Reaching the open valley floor at the bottom of the slope, he gave Colonel Ben his head and hung on. They entered the timber on the other side long before the raiders came over the ridge. The horse wasn't even breathing hard.

The ground was higher. The timber thicker. The sun was getting low. Purcell was sure he had lost them. He found a grass-covered opening ringed by brush. He slipped off the horse's back and opened the potato sack.

The horse eagerly began to graze. Squatting, Purcell held the picket rope and munched on a potato. It was crisp and tasted good. He would find something else tomorrow. He knew he would soon tire of raw potato.

The buckskin jacket felt good against the evening's damp chill. Eppie had made it for him two years ago. He and Gran had scraped and tanned the deer hide themselves. She had made it much too large. Her explanation was that it would last a long time, and he would grow into it. Although it was still a little too large, he realized he was beginning to fill it out.

The jacket, the red flannel shirt he wore, and the jackknife in his pocket was all he had to remember

Eppie by. In the hours since the killings he had rec-
onciled to the fact that Granville and Eppie were
gone. He was alone again.

The incident of the jackknife amused him.
Like most youngsters he heard and saw a lot more
than the adults realized. He recalled that he was sitting on the stairs leading to the loft, when the conversation drifted around the corner...

It was his first Christmas with them. Eppie
asked, "Granville, what are you going to give Stephen
for Christmas?"

His uncle had grumbled, "Nothing. I'm giving him a home, and teaching him a man's ways.
He's a good boy, that's all he will need."

"Now Granville, the boy follows you around
like a hound pup. He hangs on to every word you say.
There should be something from you Christmas
morning."

"If you say so," he said. "What should I fix
up?"

"Nothing, I took care of it. I bought a jackknife at the hardware store. The boy should be carrying something like that instead of a butcher knife in
his belt, like a half-wild savage. Now, when he gets
the knife, you just act like you knew all about it."

The old man did too, saying proudly, "That's
a good one. It's a Barlow."

Granville and Eppie had treated Purcell well. He knew he had became the child they never had. Granville Coldiron was a great-uncle, the older brother of Purcell's mother's father.

Purcell's mother died shortly after his birth in New York. His father was a sea captain, and left the baby with his maiden sister. When Purcell was ten years old, she succumbed to the ague. His father placed him in a private boarding school to prepare him for application to a military school.

Young Stephen Purcell was a bright student, full of energy that sometimes brought him trouble. Tall with dark hair, Stephen looked older than he was. The headmaster decided he needed something in addition to his studies to keep him busy. He was hired out to a telegraph office as an office boy.

In a few weeks time, Purcell had learned to use the telegraph. He worked as a part time operator. He became familiar with the sending and receiving equipment. He studied the maintenance of the batteries and wires. Purcell was all eyes and ears when the line construction and maintenance crews were in the office. He occasionally went to the construction site with them.

It was shortly after Purcell's fifteenth birthday when the headmaster called him to the office and gravely informed him of his father's death. His father's ship was believed to have gone down in a storm off the coast of South America near Cape Horn.

Knowing that the money for schooling would soon run out, the headmaster quizzed the boy about relatives. He found that Stephen Purcell had few known relatives, the closest being an older brother to Purcell's mother. The uncle was, or had been, a politician that had resigned his office and went west with the forty-niners seeking his fortune in California. He had not been heard from for many years.

The other relative was an older brother to Stephen's mother's deceased father. That uncle was living in the Shenandoah Valley near Cross Keys, and Port Republic. The headmaster wrote to Granville and Eppie Coldiron, inquiring what he should do with the orphaned boy. The response came back with a bank draft, along with instructions on how to send the boy by railroad. Granville and Eppie met him at the railroad station at Mt. Jackson.

They traveled to the farm in a carriage behind a team of horses. Staying overnight in New Market, they arrived at Granville and Eppie's home late the next day.

When Stephen Purcell awoke the next morning, he realized he was in a strange and entirely different world than he had known before.

The farm was located among rolling hills, close to the mountainous area on the East side of the

Shenandoah Valley. It consisted of rail-fenced fields, pasture, and timber. A large barn housed the horses and mules. Breeding pens and sheds were located on another run, a little farther from the main buildings. Other stables with smaller sheds and buildings for cattle and swine were located in an opposite direction. The Coldirons were traditionally a family of blacksmiths, so there was a blacksmith shop and a carpenter's shop. A rock-walled flower garden, and a large vegetable garden completed the farmstead.

The first floor walls of the house were made of logs. There was an opening in the center with a flagstone floor, commonly called a dogtrot. The second floor, constructed of board and batten, contained the sleeping rooms.

Three log-and-board cabins located to the side of the yard made living quarters for the stock handlers and field hands. It looked nothing like the New York City streets Purcell was familiar with. He knew he would hate the farm, and had decided to leave as soon as he could.

It didn't happen that way. He had liked the valley, the mountains, the farm, and the work that came with it all. He helped train and care for the horses and mules. The colt they called Colonel Ben became his constant companion.

Colonel Ben snorted, interrupting Purcell's thoughts. Darkness had closed in around him. The Reb raiders would be around their cooking fires now. It was time to move.

Chapter 2

Lighting flashed farther south in the valley, and the ominous sound of thunder rolled overhead as Purcell made his way off the west slope of the Blue Ridge. He skirted around Conrad's Store, remembering that Jackson's forces had burned the bridge there two years before.

He arrived at a low water crossing to find the river rising from the rains upstream. Ben waded through and they struck west. A short time later he found the Keezletown road. Just outside Keezletown a driving rain boiled up out of the south and completely soaked him in seconds.

He caught a glimpse of some buildings, and decided to ride straight through on the road instead of trying to negotiate unfamiliar terrain in the dark and rain.

The storm lashed out at them. Water ran into Purcell's eyes and nose. The horse tried to stop and turn his rump to the wind. Purcell urged the horse on.

Finally the rain slowed. He left the road, intending to cross the Port Republic and Mt. Crawford roads. He would cross the Valley Pike south of Harrisonburg, and strike for West Virginia. With luck he would be across the Pike before daylight.

Before he approached the Pike the rain started again. The horse picked his way through some trees and out onto the road. The wind and thunder were deafening. He wiped the rain from his eyes. He thought he heard a voice. The lighting flashed, and Purcell discovered he was in the middle of a Confederate supply train. Several men were shoving on a mired wagon. The team of horses were spooking in the storm, and were see-sawing back and forth instead of pulling together. Riders were coming toward him.

Purcell fought the impulse to run. He decided to bluff his way through. Skirting the wagon, he pushed the horse south on the road going on by the first pair of cavalrymen. Suddenly he was face on with a young Confederate officer. "Say fellow, why didn't you help with the stuck wagon?"

"It was almost free," Purcell answered calmly.

He was a hundred yards past them, and moving out at a brisk trot when he heard the sound of horses running in the mud.

"Halt! Stop that rider! He's riding bareback. There is something wrong here."
Purcell turned left, back into the trees the way he had came. Through the trees he struck open meadow, and let the horse run. They were on him, and coming hard. Every time the lighting flashed one or two shots rang out. He prayed that they wouldn't hit the horse.

The ditch! It was there somewhere, he had crossed it on his approach to the road. He found it and jumped the horse across. There was nothing but open meadow in front and on both sides. All they had to do was stand, and shoot at him each time the lighting flashed. He didn't have a chance. What would Granville do? In the same thought he answered his own question. The buffalo wallow story! He raced back to the ditch. Jumping off Colonel Ben, he led him into the muddy break. It was five to six feet wide, and four foot deep. Would the horse go down? He had to. Purcell grabbed the horse's left front foot and folded it back. He kicked at the other front foot. The horse obediently went to his knees.

Purcell shoved desperately on the big horse, and he flopped over on his side.

Quickly, using a rein, he tied the folded left foot back against the foreleg. He gently held the horse's head down.

"Hell, I saw him jump the ditch. He's out there somewhere.

"Who do you reckon he is?"

"I don't know, but he didn't belong where he was. He was riding bareback. The lieutenant thinks he was a youngster. Probably a deserter. Stole a horse, and is going home to his mommy."

After a time, they moved on. Purcell waited, and mentally ticked off fifteen to twenty minutes. He pulled the knot loose and let the horse up. He started south in the ditch walking ahead of the horse for several hundred yards. He came to a point where the ditch angled sharply back towards the Pike. Should he try to cross the Pike again? No. He had seen a long line of supply wagons. There were soldiers everywhere. Daylight wasn't far off. Best that he strike back towards the Blue Ridge, and territory he knew.

If they were still looking for him come daylight, they would find his tracks in the muddy ditch. That was of no concern for him. He intended to be a long way off by then.

His situation was not good. The Pike was swarming with Rebs. Rebs, on the lookout for spies or deserters. He looked like a deserter. Purcell surmised that the lieutenant he bumped into wasn't very sharp. Next time he might not be so lucky.

Granville saved him with his story of the buffalo wallow fight. The old mountaineer had told of a time when a war party of Cheyennes caught Granville and four other trappers in the open on the plains. The Indians were quickly overtaking them when the trappers came upon a buffalo wallow, a slight depression wallowed out in the otherwise level prairie. They quickly dropped into the three foot deep hole.

Three trappers turned their muskets to the oncoming Cheyennes while the two remaining rigged scotch hobbles on their horses and put them down to shield them from the Indian musket balls and arrows. With the horses trussed and laying down in the bottom of the wallow, the trappers fought the Indians from the cover of the depression rim. Their long rifles took a toll, and after a day-long fight, the Indians slipped away in the dark.

The next morning the trappers loosed their animals, got them up and rode away.

Purcell marveled to himself. The story of the buffalo wallow had saved him. Suddenly, he realized the meaning of his uncle's last words... "Remember what I've told you, boy."

He was twenty-five miles from the foot of the Blue Ridge and daylight would be breaking. Purcell was cold, wet, and hungry. He would travel as far as possible in the morning fog, then hole up to rest and graze the horse.

The rain quit. Morning light began to filter through the overcast. He nudged the horse into a ground-covering canter. Before long they came to a rail fence. Dismounting, he dropped the top rails and stepped the horse over.

He rested the horse, walking ahead of him. Colonel Ben was a horse that caught the eye of every horseman. He was a new breed, a Kentucky Saddler, bred for the saddle. The chestnut's lineage went back about twenty years to the Thoroughbred called Denmark. His graceful easy way of going came from Morgan ancestry. Larger than most, he was nearly seventeen hands tall with strong muscular legs.

Granville Coldiron purchased Ben from a plantation horse breeder south of Lexington, Kentucky. He was a yearling when Granville had him shipped to Virginia a year before the secession. Granville knew good horses. He said the horse had command presence, so he called it Colonel Ben.

For the next two hours Purcell alternately cantered and walked the horse. Often, he slipped from the horse's back, and walked alongside to rest him. He was covering as much distance as he could, yet saving the horse for an all out run if needed. He heard the horse's stomach rumble, and he realized the big animal would be suffering hunger pangs too.

Just as the sun boiled away the last of the morning fog, he found a secluded draw with good grass. He tethered the horse to graze, and retired to a patch of brush a few feet off to the side.

While the horse grazed, Purcell knew he must do some serious thinking. He knew now that he could not cross over into West Virginia immediately. He must change his plans. He would lay out in the hills a few days until the Confederate troop movement subsided.

There was the problem of supplies. The grass had been slow coming this spring, but finally with some sun and the rains it was greening up. The horse was used to some grain, but he must get by on forage for now.

For Purcell it was a different matter, a steady diet of raw potato was not good. He needed meat, bread, and salt. How he wished for a cup of hot coffee.

It went against his will, but it looked like he was going to be forced to steal. He could probably make a night raid on one of the grist mills and get some flour or meal. Yet, he had no utensils and a fellow could get shot. Justifiably so. He needed some friends. Mose would help him, but it could be dangerous for Mose if he was caught.

After the raiders burned the outbuildings and the tenant houses the first time, Mose went to work for Bos Hartley. The rest of the hands and their families disappeared and went north. Mose Washington had lived in the valley all his life. His ancestors came from Africa in the hold of a slaver in the late seventeen hundreds. Washington was a prominent name in the Shenandoah then. Following the custom of the times, they simply took the name of slave owners or one that was handy. Mose was after the biblical name Moses. Stephen Purcell spent almost as much time with Mose as he did with his uncle.

Mose had traveled and trapped with Granville in the Rocky Mountains. Granville had told Stephen that Mose was a freedman, and there were papers to prove it. Eppie's family had given Mose and his family freedman status. It was payment to Mose for going to the western frontier and finding Granville, and delivering a message for Eppie after the death of her first husband. The old man moved freely through the valley, working off and on for Granville and Bos Hartley and others. Mose had the trust and respect of everyone. One of the cabins was designated for Mose and his family. Nobody else was permitted to use it. It was one of the cabins the raiders burned on the first visit.

Purcell didn't feel comfortable going to Bos Hartley's place. Bos was a friend of Granville's, but he was a pragmatic businessman. He wouldn't want the Confederates or the Federals down on him. No, going there was out of the question.

The horse slowed his grazing. Purcell went over, and commenced to rub him down. He checked each of the animal's feet, cleaning them with his knife, looking for stones or other problems. Colonel Ben's feet were holding up well considering he was without shoes.

Purcell walked up the slope to the top of the rise and scanned the countryside. He made his decision. The horse was fit to go again. They would travel on in daylight, cross the North Fork of the Shenandoah, and swing around above the farm. The ashes would be cold now. He could look for some utensils. Perhaps an iron skillet would have survived the fire intact.

A seldom-used animal trail came up out of a cut between hills just above the farmstead. Mose had shown him the trail years before. The trail came out just a few feet from where Purcell and Granville had shocked some corn fodder against the rail fence the fall before. From there he could observe the building site, and slip down to forage after dark. There would be corn in the fodder. He could husk some of it out and carry it off in his potato sack. The horse could have some grain. Parched over a fire he could eat some of the grain, too.

They made their way briskly, skirting around farmsteads, ever on the alert. Knowing the river would be swollen from the rain, he carefully picked his place to cross it. At the crossing he took his clothes off and made a bundle. He rolled hat and all inside his shirt. He placed the bundle on his head, tying the sleeves securely under his chin. With the reins tied high on the horse's neck, he wrapped a handful of the animal's tail securely around his left hand. He clucked to the horse, and slapped him on the rump with the flat of his right hand. The horse took to the water, towing Purcell.

Instinctively, the horse headed towards a partially exposed gravel bar downstream and on the far side. The current helped move them along. They gained solid footing and came out on the bar. The horse shook, throwing water from his hide. Purcell's head was still dry, as were the clothes. Purcell used the buckskin jacket for a towel and quickly dressed. Two hours or more of daylight remained. He could get to the game trail in an hour.

Mounting the horse's wet back, he wished again for a saddle. He did feel better, now that he was in country he knew. In the last few years he had hunted and fished the entire area between the river and the mountains. He had even crossed the mountains on occasion. There were some nice mountain meadows hidden in the Blue Ridge. As soon as he could locate some groceries he would go to one of these meadows. With forage for Ben, and a small amount of food for himself, he could wait for his time to move.

The thought of the meadows reminded him of the deer hunting trip with Mose. They had gone into the mountains from the very trail he was going towards.

The meat supply was low. Granville and Mose decided that a deer was needed to carry the families through until colder weather and butchering time.

The deer had retreated into the mountains because of the constant activity, and the occasional thunder of cannon in the valley. Mose thought he knew the best place to hunt but the distance into the mountains would require packing the carcass out on a mule.

Granville woke him hours before daylight. He fed Mose and Purcell breakfast. It was an exciting time for Purcell. He was to do the shooting with the Hawken.

They saddled the mules, and Mose led the way up the hill in the darkness.

"Mose," Purcell whispered. "Do you know where we are going?"

"We're a going to the meadows. Don't worry about it. I been huntin' these mountains since I was a lot younger than you. When we get up near the meadow we'll circle round till the wind's in our face. Then we'll hide in the brush or tall grass. If you got anything to say, say it now. When we get there, I don't want no talkin'."

Mose was silent for awhile, then he continued his whispered instructions. "That Hawken is the most accurate shootin' piece made. It will shoot where you aim if you can hold it steady. If we are in the timber, use a tree to steady it against. If we are in the open, drop to your right knee and steady your elbow on the other knee. Do it just like I saw your Uncle Granville showing you awhile back. Anything over a hundred yards, you start holdin' a mite high. Don't shoot at nothin' much over two hundred yards. You ain't likely to hit it." He continued. "If there's a bunch of them, pick out a young one. If there's just one, shoot it whatever it is. We need the meat."

"Where should I aim?" Purcell asked.

"If he's standing broadside, aim right behind the shoulder where his front leg hooks on. If he's close on, and straight at you, try a headshot. Head-shot's always better when you can make 'em. You waste less meat that way.

"Now, boy," Moses had said. "I don't hold with shoot'n at a running deer. Like as not, your gonna waste your powder, and lead. Worse yet, if you cripple the deer, you've wasted it."

They stopped to test the wind, and then angled to the left. Dismounting, they tied the mules in some trees.

"We'll take a place, and stay for an hour or two. Don't move around," Mose whispered.

They picked the way to the edge of the meadow, and out into some tall grass. He sat down with his head just above the grass and watched the meadow take shape in the morning light.

A few feet to the rear, Mose broke his own ban on talking. "Did you cap your piece?"

Purcell looked down at the lock of the gun. He felt his neck redden in embarrassment. Quickly he scratched for a primer cap, and slipped it over the nipple. He brought the hammer to full cock.

After awhile his muscles began to cramp, and he wished he could stand up. Suddenly five deer materialized out of nowhere. He completely forgot his discomfort. As they worked closer he picked out a fat young buck.

Carefully he squeezed the set trigger, and when the time was right he rocked forward on his right knee bringing the heavy barrel to bear on the buck. In a split second the sights were in place, and he touched off the shot. The buck jumped high, and disappeared.

"I missed him," he said, shaking his head in disgust.

"Maybe not," Mose answered. "Let's take a look."

They walked over to the spot, and then past it. The buck was laying in the grass a few yards from his original location. "A deer's natural instinct is to jump, and run. He was dead when the ball struck, but his natural reaction carried him this far," Mose explained. "You get the mules. I'll draw him."

That had been over two years ago, Purcell mused. Granville and Mose had taught him the ways of the hunter and how to shoot, even with a war going on.

The horse paused at a wash, jolting him out of his thoughts. He reminded himself to stay alert. He was nearing his destination.

Chapter 3

The horsemen stopped their mounts in the middle of the road and watched the stooped figure making his way toward them. It was a shuffling old black man in a ragged great coat, carrying an empty gunny sack.

The old man didn't even indicate he saw them until he reached them. Then he stopped and looked up, removing his hat from his graying head.

"Where are you going old man?"

"Ise going to visit my old Massa's grave," he said. "Ise paying my last respects."

"Sure you are, with an empty gunny sack. Well go ahead, old man. You ain't gonna find much up there. They done donated it all to Jeff Davis."

The old man looked after the horsemen as they rode down the lane. "Stupid asses," he said to himself. "You think Moses Washington came here to steal. Well, that's just what old Mose wants you to think." He trudged on up the lane, bent under the weight of the extra clothes and the food concealed under the coat. He stopped at the well and his eyes fell to a large tin cup lying almost hidden between two stones. He picked it up, stowing it in the empty sack...

Purcell tied Colonel Ben to a tree, and started up the narrow trail. Then, he heard the sound coming from the field above.

"Swing low, sweet chariot, coming for to carry me home--"

He couldn't believe it. Unmistakably it was Mose. He raced up the trail. Caution prevailed and he stopped a few feet from the top and gave a whip-poor-will call. Mose kept on singing. Purcell stepped into the brush beside the trail and made his way close to the fence at the edge of the field. Mose was at a fodder shock, husking ears of corn and dropping them into a neat little pile. Finally, he stopped singing.

"Boy, say something to me, if you is there."

"I'm here, Mose. You sing prettier than any church choir I ever heard."

"Stay in the brush, boy. They are on the road below, and Lord only knows where else. They has made up their minds they gonna catch you. They are telling that you and Mr. Granville was Federal spies."

"They are doing that because they are trying to justify their dirty deeds. The one called Striker wants the Colonel," Purcell said.

"Figures, they is hunting money, too. They came back, and dug through the ashes of the house. The rumor was that Granville didn't like banks, and that he had a lot of silver," the old man replied.

"He did not care for banks, but he used them. I have been in the bank at Harrisonburg with him. It is a damn mean lot that would wipe a man and his family out, because they wanted his livestock and any money he might have. I would hunt them down and kill every one of them if I could," Purcell said.

"Don't let it eat on you, too much, Stephen. They is bad men on both sides. But, they is good men, too. You want to stay a good man, as your uncle was.

"I got some vittles here for you," he said, changing the subject. "I'll leave them in the fodder shock."

"How did you know I'd be here?"

"I figured you would sneak up the trail to pick up some corn for your horse. If I didn't raise you with my noise making, I intended to leave the sack of supplies in the shock of fodder. Have you had anything to eat?"

"I've been eating raw potatoes. They are getting a little hard to take."

"How are you fixed for clothes? Been kinda chilly at night."

"I've made out all right. I tell you Mose, I'm getting mighty tired of running. They are shooting at me, and I can't shoot back. I don't have any friends, everybody is my enemy."

"You just as well off that you can't shoot back, boy. Killing people never solves anything. Anyhow, you got some friends. You just gots to be careful who you approach. Bos says your best move is to skedaddle for Federal territory. Don't go west, you are liable to get caught up in it."

"I know. I tried to cross the Pike below Harrisonburg last night, and walked right into them. If the Colonel hadn't been smart like he is, they would have got me. There are Confederate troops all over the valley. What's going on?"

"Jeff Davis put General Breckinridge in charge of the south end of the Shenandoah, and part of what they now call West Virginny. He's building up his army something fierce. Longstreet is in East

Tennessee getting ready to come down the valley. Old General Sigel's massing his Federal forces all along north end edge of the West Virginny border. This Valley's seen a sight of fighting boy, but we ain't seen the likes of what we're gonna see.

"Stephen, we don't have much more time. I'm gonna leave some vittles and things in the fodder shock. I got two tow sacks. I'm gonna leave one for you. I will carry some corn home in the other one. I shucked those cavalrymen a little, so I'd better make it look like I was up here stealing corn.

"Bos done sent you some traveling money. The cow came up to his pasture. We turned her in with his stock. Nobody will know the difference. Bos said he'd pay you that money for her, and someday if you was a mind to, you could buy her back for the same price. Don't go down there looking for something to eat. The thieves even stole all your chickens."

Mose stood up, and shouldered his bag of corn. "Wait till it's good'n dark. Then you get this stuff, and get out of here."

"Mose, you're the best friend a man could have. Thanks. I will not forget."

"Take care, boy." Mose Washington walked back down the hill with his sack of corn.

Sitting in the weeds near the fence row, Purcell surveyed the farmstead below. He could see green rows in Eppie's starter garden. She called it that, because she planted cool weather plants like lettuce, cabbage, and radishes there. Other plants were started there and transplanted to the larger garden. Later in the season she grew flowers in the small garden.

The small, raised starter garden area was enclosed by a stone and cedar fence, three feet high. Granville had made the garden for her many years ago. During the cool Spring months, a buried bed of fermenting green livestock manure warmed the earth in the enclosure. Rotted sawdust mulch held the heat in. A wagon sheet was pulled over it at night to keep out the frost and cold. It was removed in the morning to take advantage of the warm sun. When this was over, and it would be, sometime, he was going to come back and use the stones to build a wall around the graves.

Purcell watched the road and area below for movement as the day's light disappeared. The last thing he saw as darkness took over were the fresh graves in the corner of the yard.

After an hour or so, he walked up to the fence and retrieved the sack from the fodder shock. He stopped long enough to add a couple dozen ears of corn to the sack. Wasting no time, he started down the trail to the horse. Before approaching the horse he stepped off the trail, and stashed the sack. Moving quietly, he made a complete circle around the horse, checking the area out for ambushers. Satisfied, he moved in, and untied Colonel Ben. He led him to the bag, mounted, caught up the bag, and started for the meadows. Purcell was developing the habits of a hunted man.

They came out on the meadow near the spot Purcell had taken that first deer. He dropped the bags and slipped from the horse. Colonel Ben was already grazing noisily.

Purcell felt around in the bag and moved the corn to the potato sack. There was a large chunk of cured bacon in a muslin bag. He felt a small bag of salt and a bag of flour. The wooden cylinder with a cork in the end would be Lucifer matches. The pleasing aroma of ground coffee beans came from another small bag. He found a small skillet, the cup from the well, an extra pair of pants, a shirt, and a folded piece of canvas wagon sheet. Mose had thought of everything.

He pulled the wagon sheet out and wrapped it around him. Tying the picket rope around his wrist, he settled down on the bags to doze and wait for morning. He planned to hole up during the day and graze the horse at night.

Riding along the run the next morning, he found the hide he was looking for. A large tree had been undermined and felled by relentless erosion. It leaned out over a gravel bar. The branches and the mat of vines made a perfect canopy over the gravel bar. There would be more than enough room for the horse. They would be hidden from almost every direction. The spot could be approached from up or down the stream and the water would cover the tracks. There was dry fuel for a cooking fire. He could see three avenues of escape.

He moved in and started setting up his housekeeping. The first thing he needed was a decent meal. He built a small fire back against the bank and let it burn down into a good bed of coals. He cut several strips off the side of bacon and put them in the skillet. He sliced one of his potatoes, and piled the slices on top of the bacon. He settled the skillet into the coals and waited anxiously. The smell of the frying bacon set his mouth to watering. He stirred the whole thing with his knife. When the bacon and potatoes had cooked sufficiently he set the skillet on a rock, wrapping the tail of his jacket on the skillet handle to keep from burning his hand. He used the Barlow jackknife for fork and knife. He couldn't remember when food had ever tasted better. He finished up with coffee boiled in the tin cup.

He bathed in the creek, and washed his pants and shirt. Changing into the clothes Mose had brought him, he felt something in the shirt pocket, and remembered the money Bos Hartley had sent him. He dug the packet of folded newspaper from the pocket, and opened it up. There was hard money in the form of Quarter Eagles, Half Eagles, and some paper Confederate Script. The money was many times more than the cow was worth. That was what Bos had meant when he said that Purcell could buy the cow back for the same price. Mose was right. He did have friends.

He built the coals up again and made some bread dough from the flour and salt. He then fried it in the skillet, making a form of hardtack that would keep. Making the hardtack and parching some corn took the rest of his day.

He filled the empty gunny sack with leaves. When dark came, he took the wagon sheet and the sack of leaves, and rode out into the meadow for the horse to graze.

He tied the picket rope to his belt and made his bed on the sack with the canvas wrapped around him. Colonel Ben was his only salvation. He didn't intend to be caught very far from him.

Purcell woke up and realized that he had stayed on the meadow too long. The haze had lifted, and his pursuers had spotted him. Quickly, he mounted Colonel Ben and led them on another wild chase to the west.

After he was sure he had lost them, he circled back during the night. He picked up his food and gear and traveled east. He found another secluded meadow higher up on the mountain, and made camp.

Purcell hid out on the meadow for five days. He had not seen movement below in two days. Perhaps his pursuers had given up and moved on. There was some flour, salt, hard tack, parched corn, and coffee left, but the bacon was gone. He figured he had better be looking for some more groceries. By traveling north along the ridge, he could swing left into Luray and buy some supplies. He had money now. If he got into an area where he wasn't known he could buy meals, and perhaps a saddle. Once at Luray, he could attempt to cross the valley to New Market, and ride on to West Virginia. It was worth a try. The horse was in good shape, and ready to go.

The next morning they started north. Working along the mountain slopes, the going was slow. He camped that night a few miles south of Thornton's Gap.

He had changed his strategy. In unfamiliar territory he was moving cautiously, and only in daylight so he could see where he was going. He didn't want to make contact with anyone until he reached Luray.

A flurry of shots rang out ahead and he heard running horses. He kicked the big horse and turned him toward the mountains. In a few jumps they were in the cover of the timber. He stopped, waiting and listening. Shouts, a few more gunshots, and everything went quiet. The sun climbed higher, yet he waited. Finally in the late afternoon, he ventured out.

The mountain valley ahead was covered with scrub oak and cedar, with vines and heavy foliage farther up the slope. He was almost to the bottom of the slope when he saw the horse tracks and the blood. He started on, but curiosity brought him back. There was lots of blood. It had to be the horse. Incredibly, he was still running. Well shod, his feet had hit the ground in the pattern of an all out race. Purcell followed the tracks up the draw. The horse had cleared the run in one mighty leap. It had been his last. The horse lay dead in the brush on the other side.

Cautiously, Purcell rode closer. The horse was a big gray gelding. It had been shot several times. The McClellan and the saddle blanket had Federal markings on them. He dismounted, and followed the trail left by the rider. The rider was bleeding, too. He was crawling. Purcell could tell it was a struggle. The injured man was trying unsuccessfully to cover his trail. He had crawled into a thicket of brush and rhododendron.

Purcell tied his horse, and walked into the thicket. He heard the click of a cocked gun, and froze. He was looking into a rifle barrel pointed at him from behind a rotting log. "It's okay fellow, I'm not armed," Purcell said evenly. "The Rebs are chasing me, too. Can I come in?" The rifle wavered, and then fell to the side.

Purcell stepped around the log cautiously. The man wore the uniform of a Union corporal. He was shot in the stomach. He looked to be in bad shape.

"I'm finished. Can't move my legs," he said. "Who are you?"

"My name is Stephen Purcell. Mosby's men killed my family ten days ago. They have been hunting me. How did you come to be here?"

"We were ambushed south of Orlean. They killed my officer and five men. I tried to go around them at Sperryville, and rode right into the gray coated S.O.Bs."

"Is there anything I can do for you?" Purcell asked.

"There's a flask in the saddle pockets. I'd mighty well like to have a drink."

Purcell went to the dead horse and found the whiskey flask. He set it aside, unfastened the girth, and removed the saddle. He must get the soldier out of there, and he would need the saddle to do it. He took the gear, including the bridle, over to Colonel Ben. Quickly, he replaced the harness bridle, and saddled up. He carried the blanket roll and the flask back to the man. The soldier was shivering.

Purcell held the flask to his mouth. The man took a mouthful, and then swallowed.

"They caught me without a saddle. I borrowed yours. We'll load you up on my horse and get you to a medic."

"I can't ride boy... You can have my saddle, and the rest of my gear, but stay with me. I don't want to die alone. Give me another drink."

"Can I use your saber?" Purcell asked. "I want to cut a couple of saplings. I'll rig a litter from saplings and your blankets."

By the time he had the poles cut and stripped of limbs it was nearing dark. "We'll go out in the morning. I'm going to bring the horse around behind to get him in closer."

Purcell took time to go through the saddle pockets. There was some hard tack wrapped in oiled paper. He found a cartridge box containing about fifty metallic cartridges of forty-four caliber ammunition. He unbuckled the box from the saddle, and fastened it to his belt.

"I brought your ammunition box. May I see your rifle?"

"It's a Henry repeating rifle. The best made, but it didn't do me any good. I should have stopped and fought it out with them."

"I've seen one before at a hardware store in Ohio." Purcell picked it up, and let the hammer off full cock. "It's a good gun," he concluded.

Purcell turned the rifle over in his hands. The Henry repeating rifle manufactured by the New Haven Arms Company was the most modern firearm of the day. Instead of a wood forearm, a bare steel tube extended under and for the full length of the barrel.

The tube held fifteen metallic cartridges under pressure from a coiled spring. When the action was opened by a downward stroke of the trigger guard lever, the expended cartridge was removed, and a fresh cartridge fed in by the spring. The cartridge was thrust into the chamber when the action was closed. Purcell recalled one of the advertisements had stated that the rifle could kill at one thousand yards. That claim he doubted.

He released the catch on the tube, compressed the magazine spring, and unloaded the gun. Carefully he worked the action, shouldered the gun, and worked the action again, sighting in on a tree knot. It was smooth, and well balanced. He liked the way the curved buttstock fit into the hollow of his shoulder. He reloaded the gun, and chambered a cartridge.

"It works fast," the corporal said. "All you need to do is cock the hammer, fire, work the lever, sight, and fire. It will do it as many times as you've got cartridges in the magazine. I paid forty-two dollars for it," he added.

The makeshift bandage had stanched the blood flow from the man's wound. Perhaps he had just run out of blood. Purcell covered him with the blankets, and the man seemed more comfortable. He hoped the soldier would make it through the night.

Purcell wrapped up in the wagon canvas, and sat down with his back against the log and the Henry across his knees.

"Purcell, are you loyal to the Union?" the corporal asked weakly.

"We tried to stay out of it, but the Rebs murdered my aunt and uncle. I couldn't be anything else but a Federal now," Purcell answered.

After awhile the soldier said gravely, "If I don't make it...there's a dispatch packet shoved under the log. It's a telegraph cipher. My officer was carrying it to Grant at Culpeper. You can have my gear and the Henry, just give me a decent burial. You can take the dispatch on to Culpeper. That is your closest way out to the Federal lines. If you don't want to take the dispatch, burn it."

"I will take the dispatch to Grant, but you will make it, fellow. Tomorrow morning I'll rig a litter and take you out of here," Purcell promised.

"How you figure to do that?" the corporal rasped.

"I'll fasten one of those poles on each side of the horse like an Indian travois. I will sling you between the poles with the blankets. I'll pick up the other end of the poles, and the horse and I will carry you out."

"Your horse would do that without kicking my brains out?" the corporal asked.

"Yep. Uncle Granville called him a once-in-a-lifetime horse. He can do most anything, anywhere, anytime. I saw a large farmhouse on the north slope about two miles back. There's a woman there. She was feeding her chickens when I came through the timber above the house. I'll take you there. Then I'll get on the horse, and leave fast. Do you want to try it?"

"Okay, I'm game. We'll see just how good your wonder-horse is. Let's save the rest of my whiskey for morning."

Purcell awoke at daylight. He knew before he touched the man that he was dead.

Using the saber and a tin plate, he dug a shallow grave on the hillside. The effort took him most of the morning.

He went through the man's pockets, and removed his personal effects. Suddenly he realized he didn't even know his name. He wrapped the body in one of the blankets and finished the burial chore.

Purcell found the packet under the log and put it inside his shirt. He would burn it later. He wanted to get away from this place of death, as soon as he could.

He strapped the Henry and the saber to the saddle, and tightened the girth. He mounted, tried the stirrups, and then got off and adjusted them.

Purcell rode into the mountains for an hour. He stopped to make some coffee and to think. Suddenly he remembered, if he had kept the days right, yesterday had been his birthday. He was no longer a teenager. He was now twenty years old.

Chapter 4

Purcell drank the coffee and ate some hard-tack. He now had some decent gear and a weapon. The saddle and gear were marked with U.S. insignia. It occurred to him that if he were caught, the markings would add credence to his tormentors' Union spy charge. Then he realized it made little difference, they were committed to killing him anyway.

Granville, although usually outspoken in his beliefs, wanted to keep from taking sides. For his efforts he suffered the loss of his property and dignity. Finally, he had lost his life. Purcell did not know how he was going to do it, but he had a score to settle with the man named Striker. A three bullet score. Some-time their paths would cross again.

There was no walking in the middle of the road. It was a war, a dirty vicious war, neighbor against neighbor, countrymen against countrymen. He was there in the middle of it. The dispatch needed to go to Grant.

Purcell was drawn to the delivery of the dis-patch. He really had nothing else to do. By taking the dispatch to Culpeper, he would put himself be-hind the line on the Union side, until he knew what his next move was.

He broke the seal on the dispatch case and opened the packet. He would have recognized the Morse code cipher even if the corporal had not told him what it was. He read it and reread it several times, committing it to memory. Then he placed a couple of lucifers in the packet, and closed the dis-patch case. He would burn it, if he was in danger of being caught.

Once in the Union lines, he would determine a safe way to continue his journey west. It was a change in plans, but he viewed it as only temporary. The road to Culpeper Court House was as good a way out as any.

He was in the Blue Ridge between Thornton Gap and Fishers Gap. He aimed to work east, skirt around Sperryville, and take up the Culpeper road from the southwest. In the few hours of daylight left he could reach the east slope.

At dusk, Purcell found grass for Colonel Ben and made camp. He made a bed roll from the corporal's remaining blanket and his own canvas sheet. He slept warm that night, for the first time since he had been in the mountains.

Before daybreak he saddled Colonel Ben, repacked his gear, and lashed the bed roll in front of the saddle. Purcell thought about throwing the saber away to lighten the load. He decided to keep it. He took a dozen cartridges from the box and put them in the pocket of the buckskin jacket. He checked the Henry over closely and mounted up.

The plan was to use roads to cover as much distance as possible. Hopefully dark should find him between Woodville and Culpeper.

The path lay through the enemy's lines. He would rely on the horse's speed and his own wits to stay clear of the Confederates. Should he be cornered... he had the Henry.

Stephen Purcell remembered what he had read and heard about Grant. He was a quiet, unpretentious man fond of his family, horses, and cigars. It was said that he was also fond of strong drink. Granville had said Grant was a common man, with an uncommon knack for winning battles. A few weeks before, word had reached the valley that Grant had been promoted to lieutenant general. Only George Washington had held that rank previously. Now, Grant was facing Lee near Culpeper Court House, and the battle for Virginia and ultimately Richmond was about to begin. Purcell was riding straight into it.

The various wagon roads and trails showed much recent travel. Purcell kept his guard up. He spotted movement in the distance, and quickly rode into the brush to wait. Two gray-clad cavalrymen passed by, unaware that he was watching them. After several minutes he started to the road.

Purcell rode around a huge granite boulder and dropped back into the road. He heard a shout and turned to see a group of cavalrymen riding out of a lane he had just passed. They spurred their horses into a run, and started for him.

Apparently they had watched him dodge the first riders. He mentally swore at himself for his care-lessness. They shouted again for him to halt. When he didn't stop, a few warning shots were fired, and the race was on. He paced the horse, keeping the same distance between them and saving the horse's wind. He thought of the dispatch. If he stopped to burn it, he would be caught for sure.

The road came to a ridge and turned left, around the point and out of sight. On the other side he came through another smaller switchback, and suddenly found the road was tightly penned between the hillside and the river, with steep banks rising on the other side of the river. He was in a gauntlet. A feeling of uneasiness crept over him.

He looked back and saw only three riders following him. They immediately loosed some shots at him. Then he knew. The other three riders had dropped off the road to cross over the ridge, or most likely, through a cut. They would come out ahead and let the others drive him into them.

He let the horse out. Maybe he could beat all of them, yet. Colonel Ben's hooves drummed a steady beat and they began to pull away from the riders behind them. Purcell smiled to himself. His elation was short-lived. Ahead, he saw the cutoff riders angling off the slope onto the road.

He pulled the horse up and looked for a way off the road. He was boxed on the right by the hillside and the river was on his left. Dropping off the bank, he made for the river. It was no use. He could never get across and up the far bank before some of the Confederates got there. There was nothing to do but fight.

He jumped clear of the horse, leaving him behind the cover of the bank. Purcell scrambled up the incline and ran out into the road. Instantly the cutoff riders opened fire on him.

Standing in the middle of the road, Purcell threw the Henry to his shoulder, cocked, aimed, and fired, worked the lever, aimed, and fired, worked the lever, aimed, and fired again. All three saddles emptied. Purcell turned and ran out from under his own powder smoke, faced the other Confederates coming up the road, and dropped to his right knee. He aimed and fired with the deliberate coolness of a man that has nothing to lose. He felt a slap and a sting on his right shoulder, a ricochet from the road bed clipped him in the calf of his right leg. The last rider reined his horse around to run. He twisted in the saddle to fire again. Purcell calmly shot him.

Purcell stood up, slipped his hand inside his shirt, and felt for the wound on his shoulder. Luck was with him, the bullet had grazed him. It burned across the top of his shoulder. The wound was bleeding, but not bad. When he examined his leg, he could feel a flattened piece of lead just under the skin.

After the roll of gunfire the valley was quiet. One remaining Confederate horse grazed at the side of the road.

At first he was elated to be alive. The full realization of what he had done came to him and he felt a queasy sick feeling in his gut. They shot at him first. He must put any feeling of remorse aside and get out of there.

Granville had always said a man should carry a belt gun on the plains. This would be a good place to get one.

He approached the nearest downed soldier. As he approached, the Reb moved and then pulled himself up. He had a Colts Army revolver in his hand.

Purcell said, "Put the gun down. You are wounded. I will help you."

The gun came up, and Purcell repeated, "Put it down." He saw the hammer fall...The force of the striking ball knocked him down. Setting flat on the ground he shot the wounded man. The bullet struck the Reb in the forehead. He didn't get off a second shot.

Purcell pulled himself up, warily scanning the other bodies. His left side was numb. He could feel blood running down his leg. Stunned, all he wanted to do was to grab the Reb's pistol and to get out of there. Purcell knelt, and stripped the belt with holster and cap box from the body. He picked up the gun and holstered it. He retrieved a flask of powder from the dead man's jacket pocket.

Holding his side, he retreated to Colonel Ben. Purcell took the whiskey bottle and the flour bag from the saddle pocket. Slowly, not really wanting to see, he unbuckled his pants and looked at the hip wound. The pistol ball had bounced off the old Green River knife, splintered the handle, and plowed a jagged furrow across the top of his left hip. It wasn't deep or long, but it was bleeding profusely. He splashed some whiskey on the wound and plastered a handful of flour on it. The folded tail of the shirt completed the bandage. He fastened his pants and buckled the pistol belt low to bind the bandage in place.

His other wounds needed attention, but he wanted to get away from there first. Purcell mounted Colonel Ben and urged the horse up the incline and into the road. He rode by three downed men, keeping his rifle ready. They were young. Two of them, including the lieutenant he had just shot, were as young as he. Somewhere they had families, wives, and girlfriends that would mourn for them. Why did they pursue him? Why didn't they just let him go on his way? Why did they box him into a corner, and make him fight? Why must men go to war?

The sticky feeling of blood in his right boot reminded him that the leg wound needed attention. Purcell carefully dismounted and retrieved the whiskey bottle and the nearly empty flour sack. Reins in hand, he hobbled to a stump at the side of the road and sat down.

The flattened piece of lead could not be pushed through the entry hole. Examination showed it to be just under the skin of the calf, and not lodged in muscle. He decided to cut it out.

Before he could begin to remove the bullet, horsemen suddenly appeared in the road, a scant two hundred yards distant. Purcell grabbed the rifle and prepared for another fight. The first horseman threw up his hands and called truce.

They wore the blue uniforms of the Union. Keeping the rifle up, Purcell watched them ride closer.

"That was one hell of a fight you gave those Rebel boys," the officer said. "I saw the whole thing through my spyglass, from that ridge behind."

"They left me no choice, but to fight," Purcell said.

"Where are you headed?" a trooper asked.

"I'm going to Culpeper Court House. How far is it?"

"We are headed back to there. It's a far piece. It will be dark before we get in. You are welcome to ride with us," the lieutenant offered. "That is if you are able to ride?"

"I'll be ready just as soon as I cut this piece of lead out of my leg."

"Can't you wait until we get to a surgeon at Culpeper?"

"No it's bleeding. The lead needs to come out before I can bandage it and stop the bleeding."

"Okay," the lieutenant said. "Have at it." Turning in the saddle he snapped orders to the patrol. "Merkle, Smith, Logan, inspect those downed Rebs for papers and telegraph equipment. Bring back their arms and loose horses. Ramsey, Correll, go with them and stand lookout. The rest of you stay here."

Purcell made an incision over the chunk of lead with the Barlow and pried the piece out. He doused the wound with whiskey before he emptied the remainder of the flour on it, and tore the sack into strips. He wound the strips around his leg and tied them off.

In the rear a trooper said, "Did you see that? Cut that lead out like he was whittling a stick."

"What do you mean? After standing flat-footed in the middle of the road and shooting it out with them buggers, sticking a knife in his leg shouldn't bother him," a cavalryman said.

In a few minutes the search detail returned, and reported no papers of importance. They tied the extra carbines, ammunition boxes, and pistol belts on the extra horse. Purcell mounted again, and the patrol moved out at a fast pace.

Briefly, Purcell explained his predicament to the lieutenant. He detailed his meeting with the corporal. He didn't mention the cipher.

"I think they were laying for the detachment of the man you found. Or perhaps they thought you were that man," the lieutenant said.

Purcell was glad for the company of the cavalrymen. The wounds were hurting. The pain would get worse. He hoped they would arrive at their destination before long.

One trooper had been eyeing the Henry. Now, he dropped in beside Purcell. "You say that there Henry rifle belonged to a corporal?" Before Purcell could answer, he went on talking. "Well most likely it's a government issue. Let me see it."

"No," Purcell said.

"Hey, now, boy you just hand that rifle over. You hear me?"

Purcell pulled Colonel Ben to a stop and dropped the reins on the horse's neck. He pointed the rifle skyward, setting the butt against his right hip. He cocked the hammer.

The others stopped. His tormentor half turned his horse back toward Purcell.

Purcell said emphatically, "Fellow, the Confederate army has chased and shot at me for weeks. I've had to run and hide like a varmint in the woods. I hurt. I'm bloodied and tired. My horse is tired. By the Holy Man above, I hope I don't have to fight the Union Army, too."

The lieutenant broke the silence. "Slattery, you best be satisfied with the rifle you have."

The rest of them began to laugh. The one called Ramsey said, "Let's sign him up, Lieutenant Cox. He'll do to ride with."

As they neared Culpeper, the rain clouds rolled in close. In the murky dark they crossed a run, and started up an incline into town.

63

"Corporal Ramsey," the lieutenant said, "you and Correll, take this man over to Hill's mansion on East Street. There's a surgeon there. Get him fixed up, and report back to me."

They dismounted in front of a large, impressive-looking house. Correll held the horses. "Leave your rifle with Correll," the corporal said.

"No, I'll keep it with me. Don't run off with my horse," he added.

"Okay, okay," Ramsey said. "You got the whole Army of
the Potomac around you. What are you worrying about? Nobody is gonna steal your gun, or horse."

An orderly let them in. He took a look at Purcell's blood-encrusted clothes, and led them into a side room. Purcell sat down on a chair with the Henry between his knees.

After a few minutes the orderly returned with a stern-looking doctor. The doctor pulled a chair in front of Purcell.

"So you are shot up, are ye? When did it happen?"

"Several hours ago," Purcell answered.

"Why the gun? Nobody is shooting at you now. Lay it aside, and shuck off your pistol belt and your pants, so I can take a look at the holes in you."

Reluctantly, Purcell laid the rifle on the floor, stood up, and dropped his belt and trousers. The dispatch case dropped out of his shirt and onto the floor. The doctor laid it aside, and pulled Purcell's boots off. The orderly brought a basin of water and some towels. The doctor soaked the shirt loose from the hip wound and cleaned the other two wounds.

"They are a bit old, but I will try to pull them together. The leg will come out in pretty good shape. You are going to have a rough-looking scar on your hip." Indicating the dispatch case, he asked, "What about that?"

"That's a dispatch I am to take to General Grant,"
Purcell answered.

The doctor hesitated a bit, then turned to the orderly. "Are there any officers up yet?"

"Some of Meade's staff officers are downstairs in the dining room. They ate supper late, and are sitting around visiting," the orderly replied.

"Go down and get the highest ranking officer and bring him up here."

The orderly returned with a young officer. The doctor picked up the dispatch and handed it to him. "Major Forsyth, this young man had a shootout with a party of Confederate cavalry today. He was carrying this. He says that he is taking it to Grant."

Purcell watched the dapper young officer take the dispatch, and turn it over in his hands.

"Sir, I promised I would deliver it personally."

"To whom, did you promise?"

"A wounded Union corporal. He died from his wounds. I buried him and brought it on."

"Did you get the corporal's name or his unit designation?"

"No sir, but his personal things are tied in a cloth in the lefthand saddle pocket."

The officer turned to Ramsey. "Go get the material from the saddle."

Purcell observed the officer, noting that he had the crisp, professional air of command. Yet, he was very polite and personable. Ramsey returned with the cloth bundle.

Forsyth quickly examined the papers, watch, and trinkets. Turning to Ramsey, he instructed him to go to the stables and saddle the gray in the first stall. "We will deliver this to General Grant over at 'Extra Billy' Smith's mansion."

A few minutes later Ramsey came back to the door. "We put your horse up in the barn stall next to the major's. They'll care for him until you need him."

The orderly led him to a cot. Purcell shoved the rifle and the pistol belt under the bed, and fell wearily into it.

It was noon the next day before he awoke. He moved, and the pain reminded him of where he was. He sat up and immediately checked for the rifle and pistol. They were there under the bed where he had put them. A clean set of army issue clothes lay on a nearby chair.

The orderly looked in the door, and returned with a basin of warm water, soap, and a razor. "Dinner is about ready. The doctor invites you to eat with him."

It was the first time Purcell had looked into a mirror since the morning of the killings. With his long black hair and dark beard, he looked older. He wanted to look older. He decided that he would keep the beard. He trimmed his beard the best he could and washed up. Purcell hobbled out into the hallway to find where the doctor would be eating.

Chapter 5

General Grant closed the dispatch case, leaned back in his chair, and pulled thoughtfully on the cigar. "What do you know about him?"

"Just what he told me on the trip in, sir," Lieutenant Cox said. "He thinks Mosby's men burned his family out last fall and returned again this spring. They killed his aunt and uncle. He took to the mountains. They searched for him for days, maybe several weeks. There seems to be no doubt in his mind that they intended to kill him.

"The surgeon and Corporal Ramsey had several conversations with him. He's originally from

New York. He lived with his great uncle in the Shenandoah Valley in the vicinity of Cross Keys. He has been there the last five years. They raised horses and mules, and grew wheat and corn. It appears that just before the the war started his uncle took most of his stock into Ohio and sold them. The old man feared he would lose them to one or other of the armies. The secessionists took it as an attempt to support the federals. That seems to be the root of the problem."

"Does he have other family?" the general queried.

"He has an uncle, his mother's brother, on the California coast somewhere. The great uncle he was living with has a couple of brothers out west somewhere. That's all he knows. The horse he's riding is a real fancy animal. It's big, well broke, and it can run," the lieutenant added. "He's touchy about losing the horse, or his weapons. Seems he has vowed never again to be in the position of not being able to defend himself."

"I can't blame him for that. Do you think he's a killer?"

"No sir, I don't think so. He is a boy turned man. He's one hell of a fighter. I don't think his marksmanship was just luck. He's an excellent rifle shot. The old man he lived with was an old Indian fighter and trapper in his youth. The boy plans to go west, too."

"Do you think he knows telegraphy?" the general continued his questioning.

"Yes sir, he told Ramsey that he was an office boy in a New York City telegraph office, once. He has had some schooling. I'm sure of that. When he found out we were looking for telegraph gear on the Confederates he downed, he told me I should have looked at their tongues for sores or scars. It seems that telegraphers can, in certain instances, read Morse code from the cut wire by placing the wire on their tongue. I told him I was not much on looking in a dead man's mouth."

"I believe he is right, at least I have heard that before," Grant said. The general stood up, walked to the fire place, and struck a match on the fireplace lintel. He relit the cigar. "It wasn't Mosby," he mused. "Mosby's been in Fauquier County all spring. He crossed a few minutes ahead of my train at the Warrenton rail junction last week. And that's as close as I want to get to the scudder," he added, chuckling at his own close call.

The bearded general puffed in silence for a few minutes. Lieutenant Cox shifted uneasily on his feet, getting Grant's attention.

"Lieutenant, do you think he can be trusted?"

"Sir, I just don't know. He's young, maybe nineteen or twenty. He has learned to keep his wits about him. He could not have whipped that six-man Confederate detail without a huge helping of nerve. I reckon you can trust him about as much as anyone. I don't see what you are getting at," the lieutenant said.

"We have an awkward situation here. Because of Mosby's raids along the railroad, I convinced Stanton and Eckert that the cipher key should be sent by military escort instead of by train. We have so much trouble with the secretary over administration of the telegraph. I don't want anyone to know there's been a problem. Understand?"

"The seal was broken on the dispatch. I'm wondering if it was broken before or after he obtained it." Again he chewed on the cigar in silence. "Send someone to get him. We'll just ask him about it..."

"Where's the Shenandoah Sharpshooter?" Ramsey asked the orderly.

"He's in the kitchen. I've never seen a man eat so much in my life. He's as hard to fill up as a hound pup."

Ramsey went down into the dining room, and out into the side kitchen. He found Purcell peeling potatoes, and talking to the cook.

"Shenandoah, do you think you can ride?" Ramsey interrupted.

"I can sit a horse, but I don't have anywhere to go," he answered.

"Well you do now. There's a distinguished gentleman with stars on his shoulders who wants to talk to you. That is, if you can tear yourself away from those potatoes. I understand you got a fondness for potatoes. It's said that sometimes, you won't eat anything else."

Grinning, Purcell hobbled to his feet. Ramsey went out, and returned shortly with Colonel Ben. Purcell limped out to meet him carrying the Henry. He tied it to the saddle, and mounted.

They ambled north on East Street and turned west on Edmundston.

An old lady working in her garden near the street looked up and stared coldly. When they came even with her, Purcell heard her say, "You no good murderin' Yankee." He glanced in her direction, and she spat at him.

"What brought that on?" he asked Ramsey.

"Your reputation has spread. You are the man that rides a big horse and carries a fast shootn' rifle. The last version I heard, you wiped out a whole company of gray coats, single handed. Pay it no mind. This is a secessionist town," he explained. "For instance, the house you are sleeping in belongs to E. B. Hill, a Confederate officer. He's a brother to old General A. P. Hill. The people, for the most part, are polite and tolerant of the Federal occupation, but don't forget for a minute where their feelings are."

They turned a corner, and Purcell found himself in front of a house with large columns in front. Across the street he viewed the empty sheds and blacksmith shops of a wagon or coach factory. Purcell figured that this was the home and wagon factory of the stage line owner and former governor called William "Extra Billy" Smith. He heard the cooks say Smith always found some way of charging his customers a little bit extra for small services. So in a bit of southern dry humor he became known as "Extra Billy." Now the Union's top general was camped in his house. The joke among the cooks was to wonder how much extra Smith would try to charge Grant.

An officer led Purcell inside to a room where a man in a private's blouse sat behind a table, smoking a cigar. He rose and walked around the table. "So this is Stephen Purcell. I'm Ulysses Grant," he said, offering his hand. "How are your wounds?"

"Sore but healing, sir. I guess I was lucky."

"Sit down," Grant said, indicating a chair. "Tell me about your problems of the last few weeks, and how you ran afoul of the rebel patrol."

Purcell related the story of the raids, his survival and the meeting with the mortally wounded corporal. Grant interrupted frequently with questions.

After Purcell finished, Grant remained silent, contemplating the butt of his cigar. Finally he said, "I don't think it was Mosby's men. The Confederate government passed a Partisan Ranger Law enabling officers to organize guerrilla bands to forage and loot. There are several of them operating with no control. They are just thieves and cutthroats. The Confederate Command tolerates them because they need supplies. I figure one of those outfits raided your home in the Shenandoah. Mosby is the most daring and his exploits get the most notoriety, but there are many others."

"So you grow potatoes?" Grant asked, just to change the subject.

"Among other things. Right now I don't think I could plant or eat another potato," Purcell answered.

"I know the feeling. I grew a crop of them out on the West Coast in '53. The bottom dropped out of the market, and I had a pretty steady diet of potatoes, too." Grant's eyes twinkled. He seemed to find his former misfortune amusing.

Changing the subject again, Grant asked, "Have you thought about what you are going to do?"

"Yes sir, I'm going west. Maybe I will go to California. I've got to find some work and build up some funds, then I'll go that direction."

Again Grant changed the subject. "In the matter of the dispatch case you took from the corporal. I understand it had been opened?"

"No sir it had not, it was sealed. And sir, the corporal gave it to me. He said it was of great importance. He gave me his rifle and saddle for delivering it to you. He said to destroy it if I was about to be captured. I opened it and memorized it, and put matches with it as an extra precaution. The corporal told me you were at Culpeper Courthouse."

"Well," Grant said. "You have told me what I wanted to know. Have you thought about joining the service?"

"Yes sir and I decided against it. First of all, I'd probably lose my horse before it was over. Second, I've made up my mind to go west. The sooner I get started the better I will feel."

Grant stood, and again offered his hand. "Good, I like a man of purpose," he said. "One other thing, the account of the dispatch is known only to Lieutenant Cox, Corporal Ramsey, Major Forsyth, and me. You are to discuss it with no one else."

"I understand sir," Purcell said.

"Good luck, Purcell."

When the door closed Grant turned to the officer in the side room and used one of his homespun sayings. "That boy is as smart as town folks." Grant instructed the officer, "Pass the word that his horse, the equipment, and arms belong to him. No officer or man shall touch them. By my order. Find him work, perhaps with the telegraph contractor."

Chapter 6

"You are healing quickly," the doctor said. "That is one of the benefits of being young. Let me observe your wounds a few more days, then you can move on. We will need all our room here before long. Rumor has been that Grant will move against Lee as soon as the weather settles."

"Thanks," Purcell said. "I am figuring on traveling north in a few days. What will I owe you for your services?"

The doctor looked amused. "You don't owe me anything. The government pays me. The cooks say you do more than enough to pay for your victuals.

If you want to stay around, maybe we can find work for you when the wounded start coming in."

An orderly stuck his head around the frame of the door interrupting the conversation. "Hey, Shenandoah, Lieutenant Cox wants to see you out on the front steps."

Cox was leaning against a porch post. "Well, you look better than you did the last time I saw you."

"I am a lot better, Lieutenant. I want to thank you for escorting me in that night. I don't think I was very civil. I didn't know where to go, or what to do."

"Pay it no mind Purcell, you were wounded and in pain. By the way, you don't need to worry about your arms and equipment. The general personally issued orders that you are to be left alone. You can go as you please. The telegraph at Brandy Station needs an extra operator. Do you want the job?"

"It has been a while. I may be a little rusty, but yes, I would like to try it. Which way is Brandy Station?"

The lieutenant realized the kid really did not know where he was at. "Oh, it is around ten miles, or a little less, northeast of here. Tell you what, I will send your buddy Corporal Ramsey over there with you and he can get you settled in. The telegraph contractor's superintendent is a cranky old badger. He is alright, but I will send along Ramsey so he can introduce you. Be ready to leave early in the morning." Cox turned and stuck his hand out. They shook hands and Cox turned to leave. At the bottom of the steps he stopped, turned around and said, "If I was you I would not go back to the Shenandoah Valley for awhile, all hell is going to happen there before long."

Purcell figured he knew what the lieutenant meant. The valley was the main supplier of food and supplies for the Confederates. Grant was not one to fool around, and the Union would attempt to secure the Shenandoah sometime soon.

Granville and Eppie had taken their surplus mules and horses out to Ohio and sold them just before the war started. Granville had been shipping a few mules to Ohio for years. That last sale had branded him a Union man, and eventually cost them their lives.

Purcell knew he could not go back to the Shenandoah Valley until the war was over, and that could be awhile. Uncle Granville had mentioned going west, and that is what he would do. He just needed a little cash in his pocket. He ate breakfast as soon as the cooks opened up the kitchen. He had Colonel Ben saddled and his gear loaded, including the Henry in its saddle boot. The cooks had generously provided him some biscuits, fried salt pork, and dried fruit to take along.

Corporal Ramsey rode up and greeted him with a friendly taunt. "Hello feller, they told me I had special duty today, escorting one of General Grant's personal friends." Purcell nodded a greeting, and smiled modestly at the compliment. He winced as he mounted Colonel Ben. Purcell's wounds hurt, but he wasn't about to let the corporal know.

They struck north on the pike. As they left the higher ground of Culpeper, they crossed a run and traveled into a small valley. To break the silence as they rode, Purcell asked Ramsey about the Union cavalry that escorted him into Culpeper after his fight with the Confederate cavalry.

"We are a scout unit," he explained. "We were out checking for Confederate movement and locations. We were on the lookout for telegraph tappers. They gave up their hiding place to go after you. That was a double mistake on their part. They exposed themselves to us, and they should have let you be. You were more than they could handle," he laughed. "We were hiding in the brush up on the high ground watching the two gray coats that you dodged. That lieutenant that you had to shoot, at the last, was hiding in a dip up in that lane with the rest of his men. He figured you would be an easy take. You had Federal horse gear so we intended to help. By the time we got there it was all over."

"He was young, probably about my age," Purcell said. "I did not want to shoot him and I told him so. He shot me anyhow."

"Lieutenant Cox figures he was fresh out of the Military School at Lexington. He must have come from moneyed people. That's a brand new Colt's pistol you took from him. They don't come cheap. The Rebs have a hard time getting hold of them," Ramsey noted.

"I have a reminder on my hip of what that Colt can do. I wish he would have put it down when I told him to. It did not come cheap for me, either."

"That ought to be another reminder for you kid, when a man has a gun pointed at you, don't ask him to put it down. You shoot him!" Ramsey said.

Talking about it made him feel his wounds. Purcell decided to change the subject. "What about Lieutenant Cox? He seems to be an honorable person."

"He is," Ramsey replied. "He is a schoolteacher from Pennsylvania. He has a wife and young child at home. He is slated for advancement along with George Forsyth. They are both gentlemen and scholars."

They were meeting supply wagon after supply wagon. Even though it rained two days before, the dust created by the traffic was something terrible. Purcell suddenly realized that the wagons were all going towards Culpeper. None were coming back. He mentioned the fact to Ramsey.

"If I was to guess, those supplies will soon be on the road to Spotsylvania. I was told to get you settled in and get back. We will be riding lookout to Wilderness Church," Ramsey explained. "That is some of the roughest, meanest terrain in Virginia. Rumor is that Grant wanted to move a bunch of troops around by ships and march them in from the northeast, but Lincoln nixed it. So now it is a march through the swamps and thick brush of the Wilderness. Man I hate that. The Rebs will be dug in."

The land around Brandy Station was level to gently rolling, open fields interspersed with scrub oak and cedar. They passed through some pretty steep hills just before they arrived. Purcell could see the distant Blue Ridge to the west. A lumberyard and sawmill powered by a steam engine loomed along the road ahead. He saw men busy at work, making and loading wooden boats. Each boat was loaded on an individual wagon, running gear in place of the usual wagon bed.

"They are pontoon boats," Ramsey explained. "The generals expect the Rebs to burn all the bridges on the Rapidan, and Pamunkey Rivers. They will use those pontoons to hold up a bridge floor to cross on. Grant has his mind set on Richmond but he must secure northern Virginia and the Shenandoah first. We have arrived, and what a mess," he added.

Supplies were strung along both sides of the railroad tracks for hundreds of yards. Thousands of soldiers and workers had overwintered there. Mud and filth were everywhere. Acres and acres of military wagons, horses, and mules covered the landscape. Crude huts and tents with corduroy log walks were rowed up along the mud streets. He could tell that some of the troops and officers had moved out. Vacant log platforms with hitching rails through the middle indicated that some cavalry had been there. Ramsey noticed Purcell surveying the area. "Looks like you will have a hut to live in, and a place to put your horse."

"No way. We are staying on high ground. That is foot rot haven over there. I have kept the Colonel's feet cleaned up pretty good, and I am not going to put him in that mess. I also want to stay on high ground, so I can see what is around me. I will need to get the horse shod before long."

"Well the telegraph contractor will probably have a place to stay anyhow. The place has many farriers. Get him shod before long, because they will be moving on," Ramsey noted.

They followed the wire on the poles alongside the railroad to a nearby frame building. The wire went into the building on glass insulators and came back out on different insulators.

"Does that wire we have been seeing go to Culpeper?" Purcell asked.

"Yup, sure does," Ramsey replied. Sensing Purcell's next question, he added, "We stopped using it for awhile because the Rebs were tapping into it. We would find the cut, fix it, and the next night they would tap it somewhere else. Probably some of those guys you shot up. That is why your dead corporal and his officer were carrying the dispatch, I reckon."

They tied the horses to the post out front and entered the door. Two telegraphers sat behind a wood railing type barrier. One was at the sending and receiving units. The other sat at a desk nearby. Another desk with a closed roll up front was located in a corner.

Ramsey asked for the superintendent, and was told he was at his house up on the hill. Ramsey motioned for Purcell to follow, and they left the building. Near the top of the slope they came to a log cabin with a long horse shed strung out along the hill behind. An older woman answered the knock on the door. Even before Ramsey could state his business, she said, "No, mister you cannot see him. He is asleep, they worked all night to get those field telegraph wagons ready to go."

"Sorry ma'am, but you must wake him. I have a letter from the man himself."

Purcell could see the fire in her eyes. Just like fire he had seen in Aunt Eppie's eyes on a few occasions. "Corporal Ramsey, why don't we give the letter to her and she can give it to him when he wakes up? I will wait out here in the yard until then."

"Okay Shenandoah, looks like you got it under control," Ramsey said. He shook hands with Purcell, mounted his horse, and started back to Culpepper.

"I am holding a letter from General Grant!" she exclaimed.

"Yes ma'am, I think so," Purcell said modestly.

"It is time for our noon meal," she said. "Have you eaten?"

"No, I have not. You need not fix me anything. We might disturb your mister."

"It's on the stove. Ham and beans, some coffee, and cornbread in the oven. He usually wakes up when he smells food anyhow. You tie your horse and come on in here. There is a wash pan right inside the door."

He tied the horse close to the house, loosened the cinch, and pulled the Henry off the saddle. He dusted his clothes off, and tucked the rifle and pistol belt under his arm. At the door she stopped him. "I am sorry, but I do not allow strangers to bring guns into my house."

"Have him put his arms outside, by the door," a raspy voice said from inside.

The woman pointed to a spot, and Purcell complied. He went on in, poured water into the pan, and proceeded to wash his hands and face. The water turned brown. He threw it out in the yard, and poured another pan full. He washed again, even getting behind his ears. The woman was impressed. She set him a place at the table.

The owner of the voice appeared. He was dressed, but his suspenders were still hanging. He looked to be in his mid-fifties with a shock of graying red hair and a beard to match. He introduced himself as John McCorkle, district supervisor, and they shook hands. He introduced his wife as she put the cornbread on the table. He called her Liz.

They all talked as they ate. The McCorkles' questions were polite, but direct. By the time they were through with the meal, they pretty well knew who Stephen Purcell was.

Liz said, "I wondered why you had a New York accent, yet they call you Shenandoah. Now I know," she added. "You are a man alone. What do you plan to do?"

"To be truthful, I intended to hunt down and kill the man responsible for my aunt and uncle's death. A man named Striker. But, I have had to kill some men recently and I don't feel good about it," Purcell replied.

"Have you prayed about it?" Liz asked earnestly.

"Whoa," John McCorkle interrupted. "We are in a war. This isn't a time to drop religion on the man. He will come to his own terms."

Purcell found himself in the awkward position of being an arbitrator between two people he liked, but hardly knew. "Yes," he said, "I have prayed. Aunt Eppie made me say my prayers frequently. She had me read passages from the Bible to her each day to keep up my reading skills. She made me memorize the Ten Commandments and the Lord's Prayer. You remind me of my aunt," he finished, with a grin.

McCorkle nodded, indicating his approval. The kid was just as sharp as Grant's letter said he was. "Well feller, we are needing to work out a place for you to stay. I can understand you wanting to stay out of that muck down below. There is a granary in one end of the buggy shed. With the teams moving out, the extra grain storage won't be needed. Sweep it out. Take some of the lumber stored overhead in some of these other sheds, seal the granary up good, and build yourself a bunk in there. Use the soft wood, poplar or soft maple. The seasoned oak will be hard to drive nails in. But you knew that," McCorkle added.

"You can take your meals with us when you are here. When and if you are on the road, you will need to carry something with you, or fare for yourself. The stall on the other end opens up into a pen for the buggy horse. Tie yours to the fence on the outside until they get acquainted. Turn your horse in after a day or so. Watch them pretty close, I don't want that big horse crippling my buggy horse. For now it is your job to keep water and hay out for both of them. I will feed the grain. I don't want a foundered horse on my hands. Do you know what I am talking about, Shenandoah?"

"Yes, that is one of the first things my uncle taught me when I arrived at the farm. He said a horse would overeat on grain, but a mule would not. As for my horse getting along, he is even-tempered. He will probably be glad for the companionship. I can make sure they get along before I let him in. I will need to pay you for my meals and the horse's feed."

"Don't worry about it, fellow. I will take it out of your wages. In fact, it is going to be your wages until I see just how handy you are."

McCorkle had already filled the telegraph operator's job. However, McCorkle figured Purcell would be worth his keep. "There are two large boxes anchored to the wall back in the stall where the buggy is kept. One has grain for the buggy horse. The one with the lock on it is my own tool box. I will give you a key. Any tools you use out of there, you put back as soon as you are finished with them. Understand?"

Purcell nodded that he understood. "How many people have a key to the box lock?"

"Just you and me."

"May I lock my rifle in there, when I must leave it?"

"Sure, Shenandoah, but make sure it is un-loaded. Liz would appreciate if you left it there when you came over to eat. You will need some rope for the bunk and nails for the batten lath. The blacksmith shop across the run makes nails, and the sutler next to the blacksmith will have rope. I have an account with both. Use my buggy and horse and they will let you sign for the materials. And make me a list of all the tools in the box when you can get to it."

Later in the afternoon Liz questioned McCorkle about the assignment he gave to Purcell. "I thought he was supposed to be a telegraph operator. You are loading him up with a lot of menial chores."

"No, I am finding out if he will work, and what he knows. I will take him down to the telegraph office and let them check him out in a few days. If he is as handy as I think he is, I have plans for him. He may run, but I don't think so. He needs a safe place for his horse, good food, and a dry place to sleep. He is good material or Grant would not have written a letter for him."

That night at the supper table, Purcell reported that he had accumulated the materials he needed, including a broom. Liz thought the broom was a good idea. She volunteered the kitchen floor for him to sleep on that night. He declined, saying he would sleep in the hay pile so he could be near Colonel Ben. John McCorkle gave her an, "I told you so," look.

Chapter 7

Purcell awakened to an overcast day that threatened rain. The hay pile inside the shed had been a good choice. He had his materials together. It was time to check out the box of tools for a hammer and a saw. He opened the hasp lock and laid it aside. He pulled the lid up and found a wide assortment of tools. A brand new Spencer repeating carbine lay on top. Purcell smiled to himself. It looked like he wasn't the only one Liz would not allow to bring his rifle into the house.

The ring of the steel triangle that hung near the back door interrupted his thoughts. It was a call to breakfast. It reminded him of home. He picked up a saw, a draw knife, and a Roman claw hammer. He closed the lid, locked the box, and went to the house.

At breakfast he asked for a graphite pencil to make a list of the tools. Liz gave him a pencil and writing paper. He thanked her for the meal and went back to the shed.

"That boy has been working up a storm all day. He gobbled down his dinner and went right back to hammering and sawing," Liz said. "How did your day trip go?"

"The crews have got the Culpeper line back in operation. The muleskinners are rolling out wire behind the units. The battery wagons are in place and ready to keep moving along behind. They tell me it is bad there. The Federals are moving against Lee on the Orange Plank Road. It is going to be rough... I think I should check up on the kid."

"John, that boy is a man. He has seen things. He has done things a kid doesn't do. Here is your list. He left it with me at noon. How does he know the names of all those tools?" she asked.

McCorkle reviewed the list. He smiled to himself. Purcell was smart enough not to list the Spencer. "He writes well and he correctly listed all the telegraph equipment, including the climbing hooks. He listed six carpenter planes of various types and one plow plane. He listed the saws and hammers correctly. He calls one hammer a leather hammer. That must be that funny looking hammer. I didn't know what it was," he mused. "He called the wood chisels and gouges right, also."

"John McCorkle, you knew that all those tools were there. You were just testing that young man," Liz said.

In answer to her first question, McCorkle said, "He probably remembered the telegraph equipment from his schooling in New York City. He worked as an office boy in a telegraph office there. The time he spent with the old mountain man uncle has been good for him. The boy says the old man could do about anything. He even had his own farm blacksmith shop, until they raided him. The kid–er young man– said the foragers carried off everything but the anvil. He said they tried, but it was too big for them to carry horseback. And yes, I was testing him and keeping him occupied. When do you want me to tell him to come to supper?"

"I will feed you both in about half an hour," Liz instructed. "I have been holding supper off 'til you got home."

"Well, Shenandoah, you have been busy. Looks good. Liz gave me your tool list. I bought that batch of carpenter's tools from the guy I had build the cabinets in the house and these grain boxes. He was getting homesick and needed money to go back to Pennsylvania. By the way, what is a leather hammer used for?"

"The leather hammer has a large head with a convex or slightly rounded face. When a cobbler or saddler pounds in pegs or tacks, the hammer doesn't mark or imprint the leather. I imagine the carpenter was using it on finish work, in much the same way," Purcell explained.

"Well I would have never thought of that!" McCorkle exclaimed.

"I don't think he would have known much about electromagnetic receiving units either," Purcell offered.

"There is one thing I have been meaning to tell you," McCorkle said. "You should hunt up a different saddle blanket, and scrape the other USA markings off your saddle. Be sure and cut the flap off your pistol holster. Replace the buckle with a plain harness buckle. They are marked CSA and that could get you some trouble for sure."

"Thanks," Purcell said. "I hadn't thought that far ahead."

"Tomorrow we will go over to the general store and get you a couple pair of canvas pants. Those wool pants aren't going to stay together very long. Lets go get cleaned up for supper." As McCorkle turned to leave, he told himself that he may have found the right-hand man that he had been wishing for.

The next day Purcell finished a wood bunk. He used the drill and auger bit to bore equally spaced holes along the side and end rails. He laced the rope he had purchased back and forth, end to end, and side to side. Liz sewed up a canvas tick the size of the bunk. Purcell filled it with straw to finish the bed. He had a place of his own again. At least for a little while.

McCorkle took him to the telegraph office, and gave them instructions to let him observe and use the equipment. The senior operator's name was Adams. The new man's name was Williams. Adams needed sleep and turned it over to Williams. Williams was nervous about his job, and would not offer the key to Purcell. Purcell watched the operation all day. He knew he could still do it.

The next morning, Adams put him in front of the equipment and promptly stretched out on the bench for a nap. Williams had apparently been instructed not to report for duty until noon. McCorkle had been quick to see the problem and act on it. Purcell was soon relaying, sending, and receiving as he had years before.

McCorkle came in about noon and woke Adams up. He took Adams outside. Purcell knew the conversation would be about him. They came back in. McCorkle told Purcell to come to the cabin for dinner as soon as Williams reported in.

McCorkle explained as they ate, "Adams said you could do the job. That is all I needed to know. Adams is working at night. Williams works the day shift. A third operator comes in, when called for. They work long hours. Adams draws thirty-five dollars a month, and Williams makes thirty dollars. I will start you at twenty-five dollars and found for you, including your horse. If you work out I will pay more. They don't need you and I do."

"What do you have in mind?" Purcell inquired. The found sounded good to him.

"I want you to ride with me. You will run errands for me, do line repair, and guard duty. We will give your wounds a few more days to heal before you go to work."

"That suits me. I wasn't pining to be tied down to a telegraph key anyhow," Purcell replied. "Although it is probably good pay," he quickly added.

After they had finished the noon meal, Purcell went over to the harness storage shed and looked around for leather scraps and sewing supplies. He knew that he could not wear the pistol belt over his hip wound. If he wanted to travel armed, he must devise a way of holstering the Colt differently. He found an awl and a partial spool of cotton string on the work bench. The harness maker had even left a ball of beeswax to wax up the string. Granville was not the only one who did that, he mused to himself.

Purcell fashioned a shoulder supported holster from the cut-down Confederate's holster. The gun would hang just above the hip and under his left arm. Supported by a wide band over the shoulder, a narrow strap around the rib cage would hold it in place. He had seen such gun holsters worn by detectives in New York City. With modifications to his shirt to hide the chest strap, he could wear the Colt under his jacket unobtrusively. It took him all afternoon to finish the project to his satisfaction.

That evening he reported to McCorkle that he was working on leather goods, and would be glad to work on any harness and saddles that needed attention. McCorkle gave him a McClellan saddle and Liz's sidesaddle to work on.

"The McClellan needs the toe shields replaced on the stirrups, and the sidesaddle needs the leg rest recovered. You can purchase some glove leather for the sidesaddle horn, over at the general store."
McCorkle later told Liz, "The guy looks for something to do. That is good."

The next morning Purcell saddled Colonel Ben for the short ride to the store. He left the Henry in the box, but he strapped the Colt under his arm and put his jacket on. He rode Ben down the slope and picked up the road through town. The town was almost deserted. One horse was tied in front of the store. Purcell tied Ben to the other end of the hitching rail and went in. Purcell watched the owner of the horse purchase some salt pork and hardtack crackers. The man asked the storekeeper for the best road to take west and avoid Confederate-held territory.

Purcell caught his breath. The voice belonged to the raider that had been across the rock fence the day Granville and Eppie were killed. He stood stunned as the man paid for the groceries, walked by him, and out the door.

Purcell ran for the door, jerking the Colt as he ran. The man mounted, and looked up to find that he was facing a gun. He showed little surprise, if any.

"Be careful with that thing feller, it might go off," he said calmly.

"It will, when I want it to," Purcell answered. "You don't know me, but we have a score to settle."

"You may be right about a score, mister. But you are wrong, I do know you. You are wearing the same red shirt you were wearing when I spotted you through the rock fence and blocked the view from the other guy."

After a pause he continued, "Do what you want to do, I am leaving this miserable war and going back to Kentucky. I never signed on to rob and kill innocent people." He turned his horse to go.

"Wait a minute," Purcell said. "I believe you, and as far as my concern we are even. I would like to know where Striker is?"

The Kentuckian turned his horse back. This time he did not look at Purcell. "He is still murdering and thieving around Cedar Creek. He has even been down to Thornton Gap, and over around Culpeper. He don't get around Cross keys anymore. The people there don't like him. He got too much notoriety when he killed your old uncle and had us chasing you all over hell. I quit him a couple weeks ago, so I don't know where he is now. He makes forays into Southern Pennsylvania. There's more money there."

"What is his full name, and how can I recognize him?" Purcell asked.

"Alvin Striker. He was a horse thief from Tennessee. Went to the war to avoid the law. They made him a lieutenant under the Jeff Davis Partisan Ranger Law. He is a mean feller. He would just as soon put a bullet in your back or a knife in your belly as to look at you. Sometimes he wears a beard, and sometimes he don't. He had heard your uncle didn't like banks. Striker thought you were carrying your uncle's stash in a poke when you ran. That is why he had us chasing you all over the mountains for days. He said he wanted your horse, but it was money he was after. That is about all I know, or care to remember." He looked Colonel Ben over. "I see you still have your Kentucky Saddler," he added.

"What is your name?" Purcell asked.

"Other than the nickname they gave you, I don't know your name, and I don't want you to know mine."

"Okay, if that is the way you want it. I wish you a safe trip back to Kentucky."

Purcell watched the disillusioned Rebel deserter ride on down the street. He turned to go back into the store. He found the storekeeper observing from the doorway. "Seems like you must have had a run in with that feller sometime."

"Last month he was with some Confederate raiders that killed my aunt and uncle over in the valley. He didn't participate in the killing. It appears he is deserting," Purcell explained.

"So I heard. You did the right thing by not shooting him," the storekeeper replied. "Now, would you mind putting your gun away?"

Purcell ducked his head, embarrassed. "I am sorry, sir. I just could not let him go without finding out something. Have you heard of Alvin Striker?"

"Yes, I have heard the troops talk a lot about Striker, and Mosby, and McNeil, among others. They hate Striker, and have some respect for Mosby and McNeil. They want to capture Mosby and shoot Striker. That ought to tell us something. Don't you think?"

Purcell and the storekeeper went back inside. Purcell finished his purchases. He returned to the harness shop and went to work on the saddles. When the wind was in the east, he could hear the distant thunder of cannon fire.

Liz struck the triangle for dinner.

After he finished the meal, Purcell took a pan of hot water out on the back step and proceeded to dress the hip wound. Liz appeared, and demanded to examine the wound. Reluctantly, he let her look at it. "There is something in there!" she exclaimed.

"It is a sliver from the knife handle." He explained further. "The doctor in Culpeper told me that if one was in there, it would work to the surface, and that I should watch the wound closely. The doctor said he did not want to cut the sliver out and risk damaging more muscle tissue."

Liz decided to intervene. "I can see the end of the sliver and I am going to take it out. It is time that thing was healing up." She disappeared into the cabin, and returned with a small sharp-pointed knife.

"I sterilized the point in the fire. As soon as it is cool, I will dip the point under the sliver and pull it out." She did just that and finished cleaning the wound. "There," she said. "Unless there is another one in there it should heal quickly." Bless Liz, she had taken over for Eppie, he mused to himself.

McCorkle returned in the evening just before supper. He mentioned that he had stopped at the telegraph office and there was a telegram from one of Sheridan's staff officers. "They are requesting that I send the telegraph man called Shenandoah to perform some special contract work."

"John McCorkle, you surely are not going to send that boy back into the fray," Liz scolded. "His hip wound is still weeping. He won't be so lucky next time. Tell them immediately you are not going to send him."

"Now, now, get off your high horse. I sent them a return telegram telling them he was not up to field work yet. Sheridan is a rough rider. Someone on Sheridan's staff knows the boy is sharp and gutsy. I figure they have something cooking..." This time Liz did not scold him for calling Purcell a boy.

At the supper table McCorkle asked Purcell if he knew a Major Forsyth on General Sheridan's staff. "I met a Major Forsyth," answered Purcell. "He was staying at the Hill Mansion in Culpeper. However, he was on Meade's staff."

"Which one? There are two of them."

"This officer's first name was George." Purcell was puzzled, and asked, "Do you know him?"

"I have met him. Nice fellow. It looks like he is now on Sheridan's staff. The one named James Forsyth is Sheridan's chief of staff. I don't think the two Forsyths are related. Anyhow, the one named George sent me a telegram asking how you were getting along."

Purcell thought that it was a strange incident and an awkward conversation. He figured that McCorkle would explain further if needed.

McCorkle picked up his coffee cup and took a sip. He turned to watch Liz as she stepped out the back door with a couple of wet dishtowels. He knew she was going to the backyard clothesline. When the door closed, he turned back to Purcell. Looking at Purcell over the coffee cup he said, "I stopped by the store this afternoon. The store keeper told me you threw down on a Confederate deserter today."

"He was with the raiders that killed my family. I wanted to talk to him," Purcell answered. "I found out the leader's full name and where he is operating. This guy didn't participate in the killing. I heard him voice objections to it that day. So I let him go."

"You got to be careful, son. For all you know, he may have let you go," McCorkle said.

McCorkle changed the subject when Liz came back into the room, asking Purcell if he was up to driving a team. "A stray Confederate cannonball fell onto a telegraph wagon near Wilderness Tavern," he explained. "It blew the wagon to pieces. Luckily, the operator had just stepped out of the wagon. We need to get another wagon to the rear of the troops. You will be traveling with two other freight wagons, each loaded with four 200 pound spools of insulated wire. I must stay close to the telegraph and the supply depot." McCorkle continued, "I would like to go with you on this first run, but I will not leave Liz alone here at night now that the troops have left."

"I am ready to go. It is time I started earning my money," Purcell replied.

"Get a bedroll and gear together. Take your saddle. You can ride one of the team horses back should the teamsters not come back with you. A field telegraph crew will meet you near Wilderness Tavern, at the intersection of the Germanna Plank road and the Orange Turnpike. The black horse is an easy rider."

"Will we be traveling with a supply caravan?" Purcell asked.

"You will probably pick one up at Culpeper. Supplies were stockpiled there before the temporary

Germanna Ford Bridge across the Rapadan was constructed. We will eat breakfast early and meet up with the wire wagons at the railroad siding. It should take about a day to get there and most of a day to get back"

Purcell said goodnight and returned to his quarters. It did not take long for him to get his gear together. As he lay in his bunk, he ran the next day's work through his mind. He recalled Grant's comments about the Confederate Partisan Ranger Law. The Brandy Station to Culpeper telegraph lines had been tapped repeatedly by Reb operatives. Civilian telegrams were not coded. Purcell was suddenly uneasy. He would ask about a military escort.

At breakfast it was evident that McCorkle did not want to discuss the day's work. Liz did not say much either. When he got up to leave she handed Purcell a flour bag with some fried sausage and egg sandwiches, and a water canteen. On the way to the horse stalls, Purcell asked if Liz was okay.

"I been wanting her to return to our home in Pennsylvania. She came to spend the winter with me. Now, she doesn't want to go back. As long as there was Federal Troops all over the place, I figured it was safe. Now I am not so sure. I have told her she must go back. She is not very happy with me."

"I think you are right. The Rebs that tapped your lines were coming out of the Shenandoah and the Blue Ridge. According to General Grant, there are more than a few Reb raider groups at work. Which brings me to a question I wanted to ask," Purcell said. "Will we have a military escort today?"

"No, I asked for one. They did not think we needed an escort for three wagons. Translated, that means they did not have the men to spare. I have armed all the four teamsters with Spencer carbines. Murphy, Bean, and Smith are experienced with weapons. I don't think Farley is," McCorkle related. "All four have been to Wilderness Tavern," he added.

"Who is in charge?" Purcell asked.

"I thought you knew. You are."

"Do they know that?"

"Not yet," McCorkle replied. "When you get down there, arrange the wagons how you want them. That will be a good way to get the point across. Murphy is usually the construction crew boss. You are the wagon boss, calling the shots on this trip. He may not like it at first. But, he is a good hand. He will come around. Stay close to him, in case you need his help."

That was a good suggestion, and Purcell already knew how he wanted the wagons to travel.

When they reached the railroad siding he pulled the telegraph wagon around in front of the two wire wagons.

McCorkle introduced Purcell, saying he would be the wagon boss for the trip. "Gentlemen, I know you think he is young, but he has three Reb bullet holes in him and in my book that makes him a man. Purcell, do you have any thing you want to tell them?"

Purcell stepped forward and said, "We will travel in the order we are in now and we will stay as close together as we can. If we have trouble, it will come from behind. If they hit us, it will more than likely be a small bunch. We won't be able to outrun them, so we must fort up and fight from the cover of the wagons."

"Pshaw, there ain't nobody gonna attack us, boy."

"Whats your name, feller?" Purcell asked.

"Murphy."

"Murphy, that is a good Irish name. You and I will ride the last wagon. Who wants to drive the telegraph wagon?" Purcell asked.

A tall thin teamster raised his hand. "Farley," he said before Purcell could ask his name.

Purcell turned to the remaining two. "I am Smith and he is Bean," Smith volunteered.

"Good," Purcell grinned. "You know which wagon you are in." Then he added, "I remember two fairly steep slopes between here and Culpeper. We will stop and rest the teams on the top of each slope. Empty wagons, should there be some, will give us the right of way. Load the magazines on your Spencers. Don't chamber a cartridge until you need to. Are there any questions?" They all looked at Murphy, then one by one, they shook their heads.

"Fine, let us move out," Purcell stated.

McCorkle returned to the cabin for his mid-morning coffee. Liz asked, "How did it go?"

"Well, Murphy usually dominates the crew. Purcell put the curb on him right at the start. Purcell is a natural-born leader. Well," McCorkle corrected himself, "I reckon his old uncle had as much to do with that as anything." He added cautiously, "I think Purcell and Murphy expected trouble. I hope they are wrong about that."

Brandy Station was still visible in the distance, when Murphy asked, "Why did you pick me to ride with?"

"Because you were ready for trouble. I saw you push the loading tube into your Spencer as I was pulling up. As I walked back by the wagons your carbine was the only one ready to go," Purcell answered.

"Yeah," said Murphy. "We could have trouble, I didn't mean to seem disrespectful. I just didn't want to scare anybody, but the Rebs have been hittin' wagon trains around Harpers Ferry, and on west of here. Burning up some telegraph stuff would be a nice little feather in some Rebs hat. If the generals were wanting to get this stuff in a hurry they should have provided us an escort." Purcell could not have agreed more.

They stopped to let the horses blow at the top of the first hill. Purcell dismounted his wagon and walked up by the first two, keeping close to the wagons. He fiddled with a stay chain on the singletree at the front of the first wagon and carefully surveyed the terrain and the road ahead. On the way back to his wagon he reminded each driver to remember to set the brake lever, and keep control of their team if trouble came their way. "Farley, drop down into the wagon bed for cover, but keep those lines tight. Bean, you bail off the wagon as soon as we know which direction they are coming from. Watch the sides, and the top of the hill for a lookout that would come at us from the front or flank. Murphy and I will do the same. We can shoot more accurately on the ground."

As he passed by the wagon he heard Bean mutter to himself nervously, "I don't know why I do this job."

Returning to the wagon, Purcell asked Murphy, "What is the story on Bean? I heard him muttering something about not liking his job."

"Bean is a good man. He don't talk much to anybody but himself. He has good eyes. He is the best shot I have seen. His full name is Horace B.

Jones. I don't know what the B. stands for. I know they started calling him Bean because he is tall and skinny like a beanpole. Smith and Bean make a good team. Smith is a bright, talkative youngster, and Bean is content to let him talk for the two of them."

They were halfway up the next hill when it happened. Five riders came out of the timber-lined creek bed, near the road at the bottom of the hill. The Rebs were shouting as they rode. They were fully expecting to overtake the fleeing wagons on the uphill pull. Like clockwork, Farley pulled the tele-graph wagon to a halt. Smith did likewise, and Murphy jammed his team up against the back of Smith's wagon. Murphy set the brake lever and rolled off the side of the wagon. Purcell was already on the ground on the opposite side. The riders were coming fast and head-on, not realizing the wagons were not going to run. Shooting from a kneeling position, Purcell took the first two out of the saddle and Murphy emptied the third saddle. The other two riders turned to run. The shouting had stopped.

Purcell yelled to not back shoot the other two riders as long as they were running. He reminded Smith and Bean to watch the timber at the top of the hill for a lookout. A second later the sound of two rapid shots came from beside the front wagon.

"Bean has got him!" Smith yelled back.

Purcell stood up and slowly scanned the area. "Is everybody alright? Farley, how about you?"

"I am alright, Purcell. The team wanted to run but I held them," Farley replied.

"Good job, Farley. Smith, Bean, are you okay?"

"We are fine, Purcell," Smith replied.

"Let's move out of here. I am going to walk along beside for awhile, so I can move either direction if needed. Bean you do the same. By the way, that was a good move you made. I worry about those two bringing help back. Remember, we stop and fight. Don't try to run. If we do they will catch us and pick us off from the back or side."

At the crest of the hill Purcell saw the downed lookout, lying near the road, where Bean had dumped him out of his saddle. His horse still stood by the body. A bridle rein was wrapped around the dead man's hand. Purcell stopped the wagons. "Bean, cover me. I am going to check your man out. That horse has saddlebags. I didn't notice saddlebags on the others."

Bean had put two holes in the man's chest as he rode at them head on. He had been a tough-looking, middle-aged fellow, with a mean-looking scar along his left jawline. Purcell wondered if someone had come at his throat with a knife and missed. Anyway, his bushwacker days were over. Bean had made sure of that.

Purcell calmed the nervous horse, and opened a saddlebag. He found a telegraph receiver and a notebook. "Farley, how far is Culpeper?"

"About a mile and a half. Maybe two miles," Farley answered.

Purcell removed a Remington .44 caliber cap and ball revolver from the Reb's belt. He also removed a leather pouch containing a cap box and lead balls. Purcell picked up the man's Sharps carbine, and checked his pockets for something to identify him. He found six 20 dollar gold pieces in his left pocket and a folding knife in his right pocket. There were six .32 caliber metallic cartridges in the other jacket pocket.

As he started to leave, he noticed a bulge in the Reb's right boot. Purcell reached into the boot and pulled out a .32 caliber Urlinger spur trigger metal cartridge type revolver. Tied inside of the left boot, he found a knife scabbard which contained a bone-handled knife with about an eight inch blade.

Purcell lead the horse back to the wagons and said, "Would you look at the weapons this guy had on him? And what about that fancy saddle? He even has a telescope in a leather tube tied to it."

"It is an officer's saddle. Looks like a Grimsley. He probably got it at the same time he came into that government-issue Sharps. Perhaps from a dead officer," Farley offered.

"Here, Bean, in case you need a pistol." Purcell handed the Remington pistol, leather bag, and powder flask to Bean. "I'll keep this fancy bone-handled knife. I imagine we better turn the horse and rifle over to the army. For now, I am going to ride him. He is a darn good horse."

Purcell mounted the horse and took up the rear. Bean mounted the lead wagon. In a short time they arrived at Extra Billy Smith's former carriage factory. Wagons were coming and going. It was a busy place.

"Water the horses and give them a bait of grain," Purcell instructed. "Feed yourselves if you got grub. If not, help yourself to my cloth bag under the seat on Murphy's wagon. I am going across the street to hunt up an officer. We will keep the horse and saddle for the time being. It gives me more flexibility."

He was not about to tell them his leg was hurting. He secured the items he had removed from the dead rebel with the scar on his jaw, including the bone-handled knife, in Murphy's wagon and tied the horse to the wagon. Handing his Henry to Murphy, he said, "Don't let that out of your sight."

Grant was not there now, but Purcell figured there were officers in Extra Billy's mansion. He knocked on the door and an orderly let him in. He approached the desk in the hallway with the saddlebags, and gave the officer the company identification card McCorkle had given him.

The officer, a captain, looked at the card and said, "So?"

Purcell said, "We are hauling some telegraph supplies into town from Brandy Station, we are to take them on to Wilderness Tavern. We were ambushed an hour ago about two miles back down the road to Brandy Station. There were six of them. We killed four of them. One of them had these saddlebags, and this Sharps."

"Well, Mr., er, uh, Stephen Purcell, what do you want me to do about it?" the captain asked, reading the name off the card. Purcell heard a chair scrape the floor in the next room.

"Shenandoah, is that you?"

"Yes sir, Lieutenant Cox." Purcell was glad to hear the familiar voice. He turned to see his friend leaning on crutches in the doorway.

"Have you been mixing it up with some more Johnny Rebs?" Cox asked.

"We have a telegraph wagon and two wire freighters. We were coming up this last slope outside town, when they struck. They knew we were coming. Your telegraph has been compromised. The Rebs knew we did not have an escort."

The officer behind the desk said, "You don't know that."

Purcell emptied the saddlebags on the man's desk. "This is an electromagnetic receiver. Two rolls of insulated light copper wire, and a pair of twisting tongs. Two graphite pencils. A notebook containing at least two days transmissions including the request for and the refusal of an escort for a telegraph wagon and two freight wagons."

Cox said, "Captain, lets take this into the colonel. I bet he would like to see this."

Purcell gathered the saddlebags and contents up. They went into the main room where Purcell had met Grant. The quartermaster, a lieutenant colonel, occupied the room now. Cox introduced the colonel, and mentioned that he was fresh in from Washington, D.C.

At Cox's advice, the colonel ordered a patrol mounted to retrieve the downed Rebs. He asked Purcell where the ambushers came from. Purcell and Cox exchanged glances.

Cox said, "I think I can answer that, colonel. They own the Shenandoah Valley and the Blue Ridge. They probably came from around Sperryville or Chester Gap. Most likely came through the Blue Ridge by way of Thornton's Gap. They may have slipped in this close hoping to destroy some supplies. We have a well-patrolled perimeter, so they hit the next best thing." He added, "In the rush of things, we have neglected to keep a close patrol on that section of telegraph line. There are just two days recorded in the notebook. I don't think they got much information. In fact, the notebook tells us every thing they got. We can be glad Purcell brought it in."

"I searched the Reb for papers or identification, but found none," Purcell reported.

"That is not unusual," Cox said. "They do not want to be identified, alive or dead."

On the way out, Purcell asked Cox what caused his wound. "A cannonball tore into a dirt and log breastwork. One of the logs flew up and landed on my leg. It is broken, the medics have it all splinted up. I can't ride. I can't walk. All I can do is sit with my leg sticking straight out. I am doing paperwork and waiting for a medical furlough, so I can go home and heal. I think your experience will convince my superiors to mount a daily patrol of that line," he added.

Purcell thanked him for his help. They shook hands and Purcell was on his way again. He left the Sharps rifle and the saddlebags with the officers.

Chapter 8

Murphy was taking the feed bags off the noses of his team of horses. He was anxious to get moving. He was glad to see Purcell crossing the street.

As Purcell approached, Murphy said, "That gray was hungry. He had not been fed for a few days. I reckon those bushwhackers had been laying in the brush for several days. I talked the supply sergeant out of a dozen bundles of corn stover. We can feed when we get to Wilderness Tavern."

Purcell was reminded of something he had heard Granville say often; you can judge a man by the way he cares for his animals. "Thanks Murphy. Are we ready for the Germanna road? How long will it take to get to Wilderness Tavern?"

"I figure a good five or six hours. We could get into a jam up at the Rapidan River crossing, on that makeshift bridge. If that happens we should find a place to camp before sundown. It is no good stumbling around in the dark. The horses will need a rest anyhow. It is a good thing that we loaded the wagons light. They are telling me that the Germanna Plank road is in bad shape. It was not built for all this traffic."

"I think I better pick up something for us to eat, if there is a chance of not making it to our destination tonight," Purcell offered.

"I sent Farley over to the sutler's store to buy some salt pork and bread. I always carry a skillet and a pot to boil coffee in. Store 'em there in that possibles box in my wagon. Smith has some stuff in his wagon, too," Murphy reassured him.

Purcell tied the Henry rifle boot on the gray's saddle and mounted up. He liked that fancy padded saddle. It was easy riding. The gray horse was not a bad ride, either.

As they pulled out, Murphy told Purcell that he had seen the orderly bring a paper out to a cavalry sergeant. The sergeant formed up a group of six mounted troopers. The troop left in a hurry, down the Brandy Station road.

"I think we can thank my friend Lieutenant Cox for that," Purcell commented. "It seemed like the other officers in there were new to the war. Cox indicated they were from Washington."

"Figures," Murphy said. "It seems that D.C. has a surplus of green officers. If they stay here and hang around Grant, they won't be green long."

Purcell found freighters backed up as they moved slowly across the Germanna bridge. They achieved the crossing, and made up some time in the flat land bottoms. The terrain soon changed. Purcell knew why they called it The Wilderness. Darkness caught them a few miles short of their destination. Other wagons had pulled over, also. Those with cavalry escort proceeded on. Murphy explained, those were probably ammunition wagons.

They attached a piece of canvas sheet to one side of Smith's wagon and threw their bedrolls under it. They led the horses to a creek for water one team at a time. Purcell rode guard each time. Murphy soon had a fire, and when it had burned down to suit him he took a piece of sheet iron from his wagon and blocked it up over the fire to make a stove. He soon had salt pork and slabs of Farley's bread on the fire. A beat-up coffeepot sat at the side ready to go on as soon as the skillet came off.

Smith had set up an iron rod tripod and had a fire below it. Bean carried an iron kettle of water from the creek and hung it under the tripod. "When you are out like this, it is best to boil all your water. You will be in misery, if you don't," Bean explained.

"Bean you don't say much, but when you do, you are very profound. Thanks for the heads up," Purcell commented. He turned and walked over to hold the tin plates as Murphy dished up their supper.

Bean turned to Smith and asked, "Do you think that meant good, or bad?"

"I think you can call that good. Very good," Smith replied.

Purcell, Farley, and Smith sat on the wagon tongue while they ate. Bean and Murphy leaned against the wagon while they consumed their supper. The teams were fed their rations of grain and fodder. Purcell asked Farley to move his team away from the battery wagon and tie them to a wire wagon. He told the teamsters that if an infiltrator was successful in setting fire to the battery wagon, that they should let it burn and not risk getting too close to it.

The damp evening air drove them under the canvas wagon sheet. They rolled out their beds, took their shoes off, and covered up, but they slept in their clothes. They kept their weapons close.

Smith asked, "Purcell, how did you know they would have a lookout posted?"

Purcell replied, "Each time they attacked my uncle's farm the raiding party posted a lookout. I expect that it is standard procedure with them."

"Do you know anything about the raiders that killed your family?" Smith queried.

"I know the leader's name. His name is Alvin Striker, and I will hunt him down and kill him, as a rabid dog should be killed."

Murphy broke the silence. "I wish you luck Purcell, but think hard about it before you start after him. Above all, keep your guard up. If he learns you are after him, he is liable to come after you, from behind."

Daylight came slowly, as the crew busied themselves with breakfast. Next the horses were watered and grained. They were soon on the road, along with many other wagons. Murphy advised everybody to stay together. "If we stop, it will be difficult to get back in."

Finally they reached Wilderness Tavern. The telegraph crewmen were waiting. They quickly switched teams, and said their next stop would be at General Burnside's headquarters.

The teamsters unloaded the reels of wire. The field quartermaster signed the bill of lading when the job was finished. He invited them to eat with the quartermaster crew. The quartermaster explained they had butchered a beef earlier in the day. Murphy and the crew were not about to pass up a free meal, and Purcell concurred.

They sat down to a table in their host's tent and enjoyed a meal of meat and potatoes. "Where did the beef come from? Perhaps off one of the area farms?" Purcell asked.

"No," the quartermaster replied. "They were shipped in from the northern states on the railroad. Drovers drive the herds along behind the various units, and butcher when required. The handy thing about cattle is that you can swim them across streams, and herd them across fields, and avoid a lot of the congestion on the road. It is a good thing we are do-ing that instead of foraging off the land. The Reb army has stripped the food supply in the whole area. I wonder what people are living on. It is bad. I don't care where their loyalty is. I feel sorry for them."

Purcell had been there and he agreed with the man. He thought it best to keep his own problems to himself. This time, he only nodded his agreement.

When they finished eating they hitched their teams to the wagons. Purcell removed the harness from the telegraph wagon team, and placed the har-ness and extra saddle in Smith's wagon. He tied the haltered team to the rear of Murphy's wagon and mounted the gray horse.

The military rule was that empty wagons were to give the right of way to loaded wagons. They spent much of the time at the side of the road. It was almost dark when they reached Culpeper. Purcell decided to camp again for the night. This time they were able to buy some fresh baked bread and butter for supper.

Before they retired to their bed rolls, Murphy called Purcell aside. "We have been discussing that horse and saddle among ourselves. We think you should keep them. I have checked the horse's mouth. He has all of his adult teeth, but the cups in his teeth aren't worn at all. That tells us he is a five-year-old. There are many years of use left in him yet. Man, you have suffered much at the hands of those buggers. Keep him," Murphy empathized.

"I will think about it tonight. Murphy, thanks for the good word," Purcell replied.

As they hitched up and prepared to start again, the depot sergeant walked over. "We took a wagon and went out to where you had the shootout. They had carried off their dead and caught up the horses. But, they sure left a lot of blood behind. It looks like you got four of them. No doubt."

"Well, let us hope we don't run into them again this morning," Murphy said. "Are you ready to go Purcell?" he added.

"I am ready," Purcell answered, and mounted the gray.

As they left town, he noticed a long string of ambulance wagons turning up the street, towards the Hill mansion. There were many parking spaces for the ambulances. As large as it was, that house would still be full of wounded men. The good doctor would be busy. Purcell didn't want to think about it any more. Smith and Bean took the lead with Purcell riding close behind them. Murphy and Farley pulled their wagon in behind. Everybody kept their weapons close at hand.

They brought the wagons into the pen near the hay shed, and unhitched. "We will leave the wagons and put the horses up. We can walk down the hill," Murphy said. "Well Shenandoah, I would bet we will be doing this again," he added.

"Wait a minute." Purcell stopped them before they could leave. He unrolled his bedroll, and found the sack which contained the belongings of the scar-faced attacker Bean had killed. Purcell pulled four of the six Double Eagles, and handed each man one. "Consider it dangerous duty pay. If an escort was with us they would have kept it. So we will keep it." No one argued with that.

Purcell dropped the remainder of his gear off at the granary and went to the cabin. He hoped Liz had a lot of hot water on the stove. He was going to soak in the wooden tub that resided on the back porch behind the curtain.

Liz was glad to see him, and soon had an extra pot of water heating on the stove. Without being asked, Purcell went to the woodpile and carried some more wood in. Later he sat in the tub and washed the dirt and sweat away. But, for the second time now, men had died by his hand. He could not wash that away. They came at him, and he prevailed. Granville would have called it a second baptism by fire. It would burn on him for many days.

Murphy opened the telegraph office door and looked in. Boss McCorkle, as he called him, was sitting at the roll top desk in the corner. McCorkle motioned Murphy toward an empty chair near the desk. "Where is Shenandoah?" McCorkle asked.

"He stopped off at your place to clean up. I think those wounds were hurting him a little. He wouldn't admit it, but I caught him favoring his leg a few times. He came into an extra horse and soft saddle. He took to it right quick."

McCorkle was puzzled. "Extra horse you say?"

"Yeah, bushwackers hit us on that last hill going into Culpeper. One of them succumbed and left his horse to Shenandoah," Murphy offered with obvious dry humor. Then he asked, "Has Shenandoah went to a military school?"

"No, I don't think so," McCorkle returned.

"I don't mind telling you that guy saved our butts. He was a step ahead of them all the way. We killed four of six. The last two turned tail and ran. We could have probably got them too, but Purcell wouldn't shoot them in the back." He added, "They knew we were coming. One of them had telegraph gear in his saddlebags. A notebook with the equipment had every message that wasn't coded for the two days previous. Your request for an escort for three telegraph supply wagons, and the refusal of an escort was there. Because of his age and appearance, Purcell figures the downed lookout was the leader of the group, and not the telegraph person. He was just carrying the gear and notebook, and bossing the operation. He was a mean-looking guy, had a nasty scar on his jaw."

"I know that trouble is always a possibility. I figured that between you, and Shenandoah, and those repeating rifles, you could handle it. Yes, the kid has a lot of metal in him. He is a thinker, too. Liz has already got him married off to a pretty neighbor girl back in Lancaster. She has not told him about it, yet," McCorkle laughed.

"Is Liz still here? I thought you were going to send her home?" Murphy asked.

"She does not want to go. Maybe this situation will help convince her. I fear that if the Union cannot push the Rebs out of Winchester, the Rebs might over run Front Royal and Brandy Station again. So I worry," McCorkle concluded.

"A sergeant at the quartermaster depot told me that they will soon pull the pontoon bridge at Germanna, and move it to facilitate removing the wounded as the battlefront moves southeast. If more wire is needed at Wilderness Tavern, it will need to be hauled soon. I think that we should use four-horse hitches from now on. Dragging even a lightly loaded wagon through that quagmire pulls a two-horse hitch something awful," Murphy explained.

"I am hoping that Grant can free up some railroad and repair it so we can ship wire in that way. Right now they are bogged down in the Wilderness. Lee don't seem to want to give ground. They will not need more wire until the army starts moving. Either way, we will need to haul some wire to the rail or to the battlefield," McCorkle explained. "Go home, and get some rest. Tomorrow we will load up a couple of wagons so we can deliver, if called upon. Have the men turn their Spencer repeaters and ammunition in here so I can lock them up."

"Something you need to know," Murphy said. "Shenandoah has vowed he is going after the Johnny Reb that killed his old uncle."

"He was close to the old people, but he has common sense. He may give up the vengeance vow. Liz has been working on him," McCorkle related.

Purcell felt better after the soak in the McCorkle's tub. His leg was not hurting as much, and he was ready to work. He shook out his bed roll and put it out in the sun to freshen it up. That was something Eppie had taught him to do.

He examined the plunder taken from the downed Reb. He unloaded the Urlinger revolver, poking five cartridges back out through the loading gate. He noted that the Reb had enough sense to leave one chamber empty under the hammer. It was a smaller revolver than the Remington, and good for a hide gun. Of course that was what the Reb was using it for.

Purcell examined the bone-handled sheath knife. The blade was razor sharp. The knife was well made. He decided he could use it. He turned it in his hand and spotted three small notches in the bone handle. He would file the notches off and replace his old, broken Green River knife. Purcell did not want to advertise that the bone-handled knife had obviously killed other men.

That ambusher with the scar on his jaw was shifty, but in the end he was no match for Bean's marksmanship. Purcell put the remaining two Double

Eagles and the folding knife in a possibles bag with the rest of his money. He threw his damaged Green River knife in the box, and placed the bone-handled knife in his belt sheath.

Purcell returned to the wagons, and began to scrape and knock the mud from the wheels with a shovel. He checked the axles and nuts for tightness as he went. In the process, he discovered an iron rim had loosened a bit on a wagon wheel. He had cleaned up both wagons by the time the dinner bell sounded.

He entered the cabin, washed up, and set down at his normal place. Liz placed a plate of food in front of him and poured some coffee. She did the same for herself, and sat across the table from him.

"John had to leave on the mid-morning train to meet one of Eckart's telegraph errand boys at Bristoe Station. I have been packing my trunk this morning. I must leave tomorrow for Lancaster. I finally gave in. He wants it, for my safety, yet he does not worry about his."

"You have family and property there. Don't you miss them?" Purcell asked.

"We have one child. A daughter. She and her husband live with us. We have a large house," Liz explained. "Yes, I miss them. Her husband is a clerk and bookkeeper at the Ealer Gun Factory. The owner Lewis Ealer died last year from wounds he received at

Gettysburg. It beats me why an old man would want to go back into battle with the militia. He had fought in the War of 1812 when he was about your age. Anyhow, the son Franklin is wanting to change the business to a retailing and merchandising establishment. Our son-in-law worries about his position."

"They will need bookkeepers whatever they do," Purcell offered.

She changed the subject. "There is something I wanted to talk to you about. This conversation is just between you and me?"

He nodded his agreement.

"You and John will be eating at Granger's Tavern. That is about the only place left where you can buy a meal. With all the soldiers around this winter and things being as they are, the owner hires waitresses and barmaids wherever he can find them. He has a couple of young girls that are rumored to be former followers of General Hooker's camps. They will put the bite on a handsome young guy like you right away. Do not fall victim to their wiles."

"Do not worry, Liz. I had about this same conversation with Aunt Eppie several years ago. And recently, I have heard all about the girls at Granger's Tavern. Nobody really knows what their history is. If the rumors are true, then I know what their game is and I won't play it," he reassured her. "Besides, I need every bit of my money. Thanks for being concerned about me."

"Alright. Okay. I was just trying to make sure they did not take advantage of you." She smiled.

Purcell excused himself as soon as he could. He needed to go to the blacksmith to obtain a piece of metal to make a shim to tighten the wagon rim. He busied himself with that project until supper time.

After supper Liz showed him where all the dishes and utensils were stored in the cabinets. "You may want to cook your own breakfast. But I know that you will both be busy," she said.

McCorkle came in sometime during the night. At breakfast, he explained that two more loads of wire would be hauled to Culpeper and stockpiled there. Eckart, the telegraph supervisor out of Washington, would order all future rail shipments to go by boat to the docks near Fredericksburg. The wire would be shipped by rail to the battlefront. He noted that Grant intended to repair all railroads and bridges as soon as he gained possession of them.

"We must move the remaining wire here, from along the tracks. We will store it under cover here for later use in and around the Shenandoah Valley. It appears the Valley is next on Grant's list," McCorkle said. "So we will be stringing ground communication line, and repairing and putting up new line anywhere it is needed."

McCorkle stood up and poured himself another cup of coffee. "Oh," he added. "Your outstanding performance saving the wire and telegraph wagons, and the lives of your crew has been noted by Washington. Some officer by the name of Cox wrote a glowing report. At my request, you have been promoted to assistant area supervisor. The pay is forty dollars per month. Don't let it go to your head. I am still your boss," McCorkle smiled, something he seldom did.

Chapter 9

The next morning, they put Liz on the train headed back into Washington D.C. She would travel by rail from Washington to Baltimore, and on to York and Lancaster. McCorkle would breathe easier when he knew that she had arrived safely back in Pennsylvania. He had an uneasy feeling that all hell was going to break loose in the Shenandoah Valley, sometime soon. A trip to Pennsylvania through Washington D.C. was difficult enough before the war. Now it was even harder.

Liz made Purcell promise that he would come to visit at Lancaster. She told him she had someone that she wanted him to meet. Purcell said he would, but he knew much would happen before then.

With Liz safely on her way, McCorkle set his teamsters and Purcell to moving and storing the wire reels that were strung along the railroad siding. First, they needed to deliver some wire to the carriage factory building at Culpeper. The plan was to have wire spotted in different locations, ready to move to the rear of the next battle site.

Purcell figured the road would be watched. He based his theory on his past two months experience. The bushwackers were there, and were just waiting for a chance to do damage. He knew in his own mind that they would always be there, until the Confederates left the Blue Ridge and the Shenandoah Valley. Purcell decided he would make his wagons look as formidable as he could.

Obtaining McCorkle's approval, Purcell put Murphy driving the lead wagon and Farley driving the second wagon. He put Smith riding the gray and Bean astride the black horse. Each carried a Spencer. In addition, Bean carried his captured Remington revolver in a belt holster. The teamsters carried Spencers in plain sight. Purcell rode Colonel Ben and kept his Henry repeater ready and visible. As Murphy had recommended, each heavily-loaded wagon was pulled by a four-horse hitch.

The trip was uneventful and the job was accomplished in one day.

The following week was spent moving and storing the remaining wire and poles in some of the abandoned horse sheds. McCorkle and Purcell traveled to Belle Plain to make arrangements for unloading some wire and pike poles from northern suppliers. The materials were to be delivered there by boat. Those materials would be hauled and stored at the Fredericksburg railroad terminal.

One evening as McCorkle and Purcell took supper at Granger's Tavern, McCorkle noted, "There are a couple good looking girls working at Granger's. Liz has almost forbid me to eat here. The way Liz sees it, some girls are like mountains. More scenic and safer, when observed from a distance. I am surprised that Liz didn't lecture you on that."

Purcell was saved from disclosing Liz and their conversation by two cavalry troopers at the next table. They interrupted to ask if McCorkle and Purcell had heard about Sheridan's raid. They had not. General Sheridan had gone completely around Richmond, destroying railroad bridges, telegraph lines, and supplies. Sheridan's men met Lee's cavalry four times and defeated them each time. The incursion had taken only two weeks total.

"That is the luckiest little Irishman I ever saw," said one of the troopers as he finished telling of the raid. "He is the fightingest general I ever saw," retorted the other trooper.

McCorkle turned to Purcell. "Now we know why Major Forsyth was inquiring after you. They needed a hard riding telegraph guy," he stated.

"If that is the case, I think I am glad I missed that," Purcell replied. The troopers nodded and returned their focus to their dinner.

"You escaped another bullet, too," McCorkle said. "I got a letter from Liz today, and she mentioned that girl she wanted you to meet. The girl got married a few weeks ago. Liz was disappointed, but she said for you not to worry, she will find another one for you." McCorkle laughed. "That is my wife. She is a jewel."

McCorkle changed the subject. "I have been called into Washington for a few days. You will be in charge. Go to the telegraph office early each morning. Check for telegraph messages from me and for me, morning, noon, and evening. Contact me only if you cannot make a decision yourself. Work at my desk part of the day. You can file and check invoices."

"How do you think the office clerks and telegraphers will take to having a 'straw boss?'" Purcell asked.

"They will do what you tell them. The teamsters and construction crews worried me, but after your first run to Culpeper, they will follow you anywhere.

"While I am out, I think I will go on over to Lancaster and spend Sunday with Liz and the daughter. Saturday afternoon, take a dollar from the cash box and pay that youngster that runs telegrams around for us. You will see him hanging around the office Saturday afternoon, waiting for his money. Don't give him a rough time. Pay him even if he has not delivered any telegrams. He is a good kid. Make a cash out note and put it in the box," McCorkle instructed.

Purcell made a breakfast of bacon and eggs. He seared a couple of slabs of McCorkle's bread, while the "boss man" as Murphy called him, packed his traveling bag. "I don't know what happened with that bread. I never could bake bread as good as Liz," McCorkle complained.

At the telegraph office Purcell busied himself at McCorkle's desk. He checked invoices and made notes on the recently stored wire and materials. He included an inventory of each new location. Storing at different locations made it harder to keep track of, but it also protected all of the materials from being lost in one fire or raid. He could tell his presence made the office employees nervous. Murphy and Smith came in and told him where they would be working. They had no problem reporting to Purcell.

After he left to eat his noon meal, Williams said to Adams, "It is difficult to believe that guy is the gunman they say he is."

"He don't carry that big six-shooter under his arm because he is a nice guy. I don't care what Murphy and Smith say," Adams retorted.

Purcell rode Colonel Ben to Granger's Tavern at the other end of town. He liked to keep the horse handy, so he could move fast if the need be. He secured Colonel Ben to the end of the hitching post.

Purcell entered the tavern, taking a seat at a table across the room from the door. The waitress came rushing by. She had two plates on her arm and one in each hand. She was just a girl. He judged her to be maybe seventeen or eighteen and she was several months pregnant. She set the plates off at the next table, then turned to take his order.

"I would like a ham sandwich, and coffee, please?" he said.

"No sandwiches today. Just potatoes, gravy, and roast beef with bread on the side," she replied abruptly.

"Okay, roast beef it is," Purcell replied with a chuckle.

"Don't patronize me," she snapped and whirled away.

"She is always like that," a guy at the next table volunteered. "She will bite your ears off and spit them on the floor. She is down on men in general. Hey aren't you the one they call Shenandoah?"

"They call me that, because the Shenandoah is my home, but, I cannot go back there. Not just yet anyhow," Purcell answered.

The waitress was coming back. "She isn't through with you yet," another fellow offered cautiously.

Purcell shrugged his shoulders to let them know it bothered him none. Little did he know.

She returned with his plate in one hand and a tin pot of coffee in the other. She set his plate in front of him, filled his coffee cup and moved on to the next table. She stopped as she passed back by.

"Well go ahead, lets have it," she commanded.

"Excuse me?" Purcell was puzzled. He heard the men at the next table begin to snicker.

"I saw you look at my belly. So lets have the smart remark, I have heard them all. Have I got one in the oven? Did I swallow a watermelon seed? Did some guy poke fun at me and I took it seriously? Am I bumping a calf yet? When am I due to pop? Who is the unlucky man? Go ahead say it. You have something smart to say. They all do."

Purcell was speechless. To make matters worse the crew at the next table were laughing up a storm. Finally he answered, "I apologize, I did not mean to be disrespectful. I did notice you were in a family way, and I am impressed at the way you are able to work so hard while in that condition. I guess I really don't know what else to say."

"Hah! Family way! That is the best one yet. I must go and write that one down, before I forget it. Family way." She threw the phrase back over her shoulder as she left.

"Hey fellow, you held your ground with her, better than most."

"I think it is easier facing a man with a gun, than a woman with that much hate in her," Purcell replied. His remark would be repeated many times by the men at the next table. It would only add to his growing reputation as a gunman.

Purcell worked in the storage yard with Murphy and the crew the rest of the day. He stopped by the telegraph office to review messages, and there were none. Adams was on the job and things seemed calm. Purcell had not planned to eat supper, but he had wrestled 200 pound reels of wire around all afternoon and worked up an appetite. Bacon and eggs at the cabin did not really appeal to him. So if he wanted something to eat, he must go back to the tavern. It was late. He figured the pregnant girl with the battery acid tongue would not still be at work. He was wrong, she was still there. She rushed back and forth with plates and a coffee pot.

He sat down as close to the kitchen as he could, to make life a little easier for her. A gesture that did not go unnoticed. An older waitress was taking the more distant tables. The girl came to take his order. She was showing the effects of the day's wear. "Have you been here all day?" he asked her.

"Oh come on. What do you care?" she replied.

"You look tired. You should sit, and rest a bit," he replied.

"We have sausage and sauerkraut. There is some beef left, and we have canned green beans," she said, ignoring his comment.

"You know, I don't think I am up to sauerkraut tonight. The beef was pretty good at noon. I will take the beef."

She brought the beef with a spoonful of boiled potatoes and a helping of green beans.

"Where do you get green beans this time of year?" He was hoping to draw her into a normal conversation.

"Granger has a lady that supplies him with vegetables. She starts growing them early and continues planting and harvesting them until late in the season. She preserves some of each batch of beans in jars. Especially the late season batch. So he has green beans the year around. The rest of his winter green stuff he used to get off a boat at Belle Plain. The boat came up from the south. The war put a stop to that," she explained.

"That is the good thing about the old string bean. They will grow, and produce when nothing else will," he noted. "Please sit and take the load off your feet."

"They are hurting," she admitted, and slowly, almost cautiously, lowered herself into the chair on the opposite side of the table. "I hear you are from New York?"

"I grew up in New York and went to a boarding school there. The last five years or so, I have lived with my Aunt and Uncle near Cross Keys. That is on up the Shenandoah River. Two and a half months ago Confederate bushwackers raided our farm, killed my Aunt and Uncle, and burned our home. They chased me all over the Blue Ridge for three weeks. They were trying to kill me for my horse."

"Where are you living now?" she inquired.

"In a granary, up on the slope by the wagon sheds. It is near the telegraph supervisor's cabin. I know telegraphy and telegraph construction. So, Mr. McCorkle sort of took me in. Otherwise, I would have had no place to go."

She locked her callused hands together and looked down at them. "Look, I am sorry about earlier today. They say the awfullest things to me. I just figured you would, too. I am here trying to earn enough money to get back home. Anything else you may have heard is not true."

"I had already come to that conclusion," he said.

"It is time to clean up. I must get busy." She rose to leave.

"My name is Stephen Purcell. May I know yours?"

She hesitated, "Helen Morley. I would just as soon the rest of this world didn't know. Only Mae, the other waitress, knows my full name."

He finished his meal, paid Mae, nodded goodbye to Helen, and left.

"Well now, I think you made a friend. I eavesdropped," Mae admitted. "If anybody needs a friend, male or female, you do," she advised.

"He is the nicest, handsomest guy I have met in a long time. But, I have too much on my plate to worry about a boyfriend now."

"How much money do you need yet, towards the train ticket?"

"Thirty dollars," Helen answered.

"That is two months wages. Do you think you will make it?"

"No, I am going on seven months," she answered.

"Granger is going to figure out before long that you lied to him about the time." Mae cautioned, "What about your sister, can she come up with some more money?"

"No, I couldn't ask for more money," she replied.

"Girl, you need to get somewhere decent to have that baby," Mae told her.

Purcell arose early and went to the telegraph office and checked the night traffic. Everything looked in order. Adams was taking a nap near the sounder. When the sounder started clicking Adams came to life instantly. McCorkle had said that Adams slept like a cat. Purcell believed it.

Purcell had not slept so well himself. He could not get the poor girl out of his mind. Once he had a chance to look at her, he realized she was nice looking. Blond with blue eyes, he figured she had Scandinavian ancestors, but the surname was Scotch or English. He knew what it was like to be in trouble with no one to turn to. He wished to know more about her.

He was already out and about, he would take breakfast at Granger's. Perhaps he would find out more.

The girl was not there. He inquired of her to Mae. "She does not come in until later. Breakfast is the lightest crowd of the day. So Granger and I handle the breakfast run. The young one puts in a hard day as it is," Mae lamented.

"What about her, Mae? How did she get into this mess?" he asked.

"Hang around a little bit and I will tell you. You must keep it to yourself," she said.

"Okay, I will take another cup of coffee," Purcell agreed.

Returning, Mae told him the gist of Helen's predicament. Her boyfriend had been determined to join the Union Army. In an emotional moment, Helen had given him, as Mae succinctly put it, "a going away present," and ended up pregnant. He would not leave his unit to come home and marry her. Her parents were uptight over her indiscretion. Her older, married sister gave her money to come out here and run him down. When Helen got here, she found he had been shot and killed last winter while on picket duty near Frederickburg.

"The poor girl is trying to put money together for a train ticket to go back to her sister at Springfield, Illinois. She is not going to make it, time is running out. She needs thirty more dollars," Mae lamented.

"That is tough. I know what it is like to be in a strange place without a friend," Purcell agreed. "But, she has you and I," he added.

He excused himself and went back to the telegraph office. He could not get the unfortunate girl off his mind. He too had been in bad circumstances, before Mose showed up to help. Purcell knew what he must do.

That night he retrieved the remaining two twenty dollar gold pieces that he had taken from the dead Reb lookout. It was blood money, and he would not need it anyhow. The next morning he gave them to Mae and explained where he got them. "It was a Confederate that shot her man, and it was only fitting that she get the money," he explained.

The next day Helen Morley got on the train. She was going home to family, and friends. She would probably never see him again, but she would not forget the man called Shenandoah.

Chapter 10

When Purcell sat down at the desk, he found a note from Adams about a wire from McCorkle. The wire informed him that McCorkle would be returning on the noon train. Williams was on duty, and at work by himself. He complained about the poor operation of the telegraph. Purcell got up from the desk and went over to the keying desk to observe.

"About an hour ago it just went weak," Williams complained.

"Does reception come back strong or does it just stay faint?"

"It has been weak on every transmission for the last hour. Since about daylight," Williams noted.

"Those are newer batteries, and I checked the acid level yesterday. This group of batteries supply the Culpeper line. It has not rained for a day or two. So the problem should not be moisture. A green limb on the line would ground it clear out, or break it down, and there would be no transmissions," Purcell mused. "Does that section of line come in from Warrenton Junction?" he asked Williams.

"Darned if I know which way it comes from. Smith and Bean are down at the loading dock getting those empty reels repaired and ready to send back on the noon train. I am sure they would know," Williams volunteered.

Purcell walked down the tracks to the loading platform and found Smith and Bean busy at work, tightening and rebuilding some damaged reels. "This line jogs around a bit, but goes clear back to Manassas and on into Washington. It follows the pike to Warrenton Junction. At that point, a line goes west to the railroad spur and on to Warrenton. The line at Warrenton Junction continues along the pike to Brentsville and on into Bristoe Station," Smith told him.

"What is at Warrenton Junction and Warrenton?" Purcell asked.

"The setup at the railroad junction depot is just like it is here, except with only with one battery.

The last I knew the line west to Warrenton was disconnected because the Rebs pretty well controlled the area" Smith explained.

"Well fellows, it looks like we have another Reb tapper between here and Warrenton Junction. McCorkle will be in at noon. We will wait and see what he wants us to do. Tell me some more about the construction details of the line if you will."

"It is almost all in the open. We replaced a bunch of poles last fall. It is a fairly solid line. It crosses the Rappahannock just above Kelly's Ford. McCorkle wouldn't put it back on the railroad bridge after they blew it during the Rappahannock Junction fight. Like I said, it follows the pike to Bristoe Station, and then follows the railroad on to Manassas, Alexandria, and on into Washington, with taps going off into the various towns along the way," Smith said.

Bean said, "Tell him about the bottom field on the other side of the Rappahannock."

"Yes, I forgot about that. There were no crops planted in that field last year and it grew up in weeds shoulder high," Smith explained for his partner.

"How large is the field?" Purcell asked.

Smith looked at Bean. "Five to ten acres. Where the weeds are," Bean said.

"I think you just pinpointed where the tap is at. I hope there is cavalry available to go out with us. We will have to go to remove the tap from the line, but I hope they will send somebody else to do the fighting."

"They won't," Bean said, in his customary to-the-point demeanor.

"Do you know anybody that lives in the area?" Purcell asked Bean.

"Nope. Wouldn't do any good if we did. They all probably lean to the South," Bean replied.

"I reckon that is right," Purcell agreed. "My experience has been that the tapper does not work alone. They travel in dog packs. One or two guys to guard the horses, and the rest to do lookout and guard the telegrapher. Where could they hide their horses? They would need a place to hide at least six horses," Purcell mused out loud.

"Every field like that usually has a cut through it, or around it. Drains to the stream. Good dirt like that, it would cut deep," Bean said.

"There is a run that twists and turns before it reaches the river. They could be working out of it. It has a lot of water in it for their horses. But, how would they get into it? It is on the north side of the river. The run is between the railroad and the tele-graph line," Smith puzzled.

"A run that twists and turns like that will have plenty of brush, grass, and even trees in the nooks along it. If the run was full of water it would still provide cover, even feed for the horses," the ever practical Bean theorized.

"They may have followed the Hazel River down from Sperryville. They could hide during the day, and pick their way along the Rappahannock bottoms after dark, and work their way up that run. I can't see how they could get by the bridge guards," Smith related.

"Easy," Purcell offered. "In the dead of night, they skirted around the southeast end of the bridge to the crossing at Kelly's Ford, and worked back upriver to the run. Now, how are we going to get them out of there?"

"Oh, man, that ain't going to be no fun," Bean said.

Smith mulled over the physical condition of the line. "We cleaned all the weeds and junk away from those poles through there, as a precaution should that field catch fire and burn our poles. The tapper won't have much cover up next to the pole."

"What did you do with all the dead weeds and refuse you cleaned up?" Purcell asked.

"We piled the cleanup from around each pole a dozen steps or so back out in the field."

"I would bet we got a Johnny Reb hidden behind one of those piles, or more likely a little farther back in the weeds, with wire strung up the nearest pole," Purcell stated. "And he should be easy to find.

It is his buddies I worry about." Purcell would not put it in words, but he did not want to put his new-found friends in danger, again. He felt it was the army's job to take on Reb troops. The army. Maybe he could work that after all. "I am going to talk to the officer in charge while I am waiting for McCorkle to get here."

Purcell realized that most of the troops stationed at Brandy station were walking wounded doing light duty, such as guarding supplies and the railroad bridge. The lieutenant in charge at Brandy station had an arm in a sling.

He knocked on the door of the cabin marked "Headquarters" and was told to enter. A private asked his name and then went through a nearby door. Lieutenant James greeted Purcell and asked him to sit. "I have seen you around, Shenandoah. You have built quite a reputation for yourself. Have you crossed paths with any Rebels today?" He laughed.

"I am sorry to report so, but I think I have, sir. They are tapping our line between the river and Rappahannock Junction. If I am right, they are working right under the noses of your bridge guards. I am guessing three to five Rebel raiders." Purcell stopped to let the lieutenant grasp what he said.

"Well how do you figure that could have happened?" the lieutenant asked.

"We know the line is being tapped. Signal strength weakened about daylight today. An extra electromagnetic sounder put online in the right place could do that," Purcell explained. "I could be wrong, but I don't think so. We think they came wide around the southeast end of the bridge in the dark last night. They probably crossed the river at the ford and went back up along the north riverbank until they hit that deep run. They are hiding their horses there. We could verify by going to the river and checking for tracks in the mud. However, we would give ourselves away and might come under fire."

"The corporal of the guard writes me a report at the end of each change of the guard. Let me re-view this morning's report." The lieutenant shuffled the papers on his table and came up with the report. "Night train came through at 10 p.m. At 1 a.m., the farm dogs down tracks south of bridge did consider-able barking. Inspected for fresh tracks under bridge this morning and found none. Underside of the bridge structure inspected and found undisturbed."

"The barking dogs back us up. You must get these guys. If they got in that easy they will come back for the bridge," Purcell offered.

"I am afraid you are right, but I don't have a lot of men at my disposal," the lieutenant said. He paused in thought and then added, "I sure would like to know exactly where they are."

"I have thought about that. I captured a good telescope during the last scrap we had with tappers. I could have a vantage point from the bridge or railroad bed, but they might spot me," Purcell said.

"There is a high, timbered hill downstream from the bridge and just south of the ford. There is a church on the south side at the bottom of the hill. We could go up the hill behind the church. I am sure we can see your telegraph lines and perhaps the creek and field from the top of the hill. If we were careful they would never know we are there," the lieutenant offered.

"I will go back to the telegraph office, to get my horse and leave my boss a message," Purcell said, as he started for the door.

"I will be ready. We are looking at about a four mile ride, one way," the lieutenant replied.

At the telegraph office, Purcell left his message for McCorkle and opened the gun locker. He removed a Spencer carbine, and a box of ammunition. He stopped by the loading dock and asked Bean if he would go along and guard the horses. Bean readily volunteered. Together they returned to the horse pens, and saddled Colonel Ben and the gray. Purcell gave Bean the Spencer and ammunition. He retrieved his own rifle and the telescope from the tool box.

At the lieutenant's command post they found him ready to proceed. Purcell introduced Bean and the lieutenant. The ride to the hill overlooking the river began. Purcell asked the lieutenant where he was from. "I notice you say creek instead of run," he said.

"That is what we call them back in Iowa." The lieutenant grinned when he said it. "Where are you from, Shenandoah? I notice you don't have a Virginia accent."

"New York City. I spent most of my life there, but I have lived in the Cross Keys/Port Republic area for the last five years. I lived with my great aunt and uncle. It was the best time of my life until we got pulled into this damn war."

"Yes, I heard they were killed by partisan rangers. I am sorry for your loss... Mr. Bean, where do you hail from?"

"Up in Maryland. War brought me here, too. I work telegraph construction," Bean replied.

After about an hour they reached the foot of the incline. At a pasture fence they took two rails down and stepped the horses across the bottom rail. They were careful to replace the rails, and left very little evidence of their passing. The horses struggled at climbing the grade, and about two-thirds of the way up they found enough brush to hide the horses from below.   Bean and his Spencer stayed to guard the horses.

Purcell and the lieutenant found a small dip in the crest, and crawled into place behind a rotting pine log. The bushes that had grown around it provided a screen. With the sun to their backs and shadows to hide them, they had the perfect observation post. Purcell immediately spied the wiretap through his glass. It was on the second pole north of the river. The tapper had used refuse from the pile to cover the wire on the ground. From their vantage point the dead weeds and grass left a telltale trail straight to the pole.

The tapper had pulled some weeds together and tied them at the top, to give him shade and cover. Through the glass they could even see him move inside his little teepee. Across the field behind the tapper, Purcell could pick out one horse in the brush. After a few minutes, two men, each leading a horse, appeared out of a cut in the bank of the small stream. They tied the horses and one Reb rolled out a blanket on the ground and lay down for a nap. The second individual leaned against a tree and seemed to be standing watch. Both would not have been visible from the pike or railroad.

"Watered their horses.   Don't you think?" whispered the lieutenant.

Purcell nodded agreement. "I am going back to the horses and change places with Bean. I want him to look things over. Bean does not talk much, but he is very observant." With that, Purcell crawled back into the brush and through the dip. He exchanged places with Bean directing him to where the lieutenant was.

After awhile Bean and the lieutenant returned. The trio made their way quietly back to the rail fence. Purcell and Lieutenant James formulated a plan to capture the three raiders during the changing of the guard, as it took place the next morning. Purcell wanted to get McCorkle's approval first.

Purcell found McCorkle waiting for him at the office. It was past noon, and both men were hungry. They ate a quick meal, and went the lieutenant's office. The lieutenant and Purcell went over the proposed plan. They would use the morning changing of the bridge guard to move in extra troops: the day crew, a corporal, and four men, plus two more hidden in the wagon that delivered the guard change. The new guards plus the night guards led by the lieutenant would file down the west side of the abutment, and double back under the bridge. If they used the river-bank and undergrowth for cover, they could make a stealthy advance on the hidden Rebs.

The telegraph construction crew comprised of Murphy, Bean, Smith, Farley, and Purcell, would leave slightly ahead of the soldiers. They would drop Purcell off at the ford, and proceed to a pole several spans past the tap. The pike rose slightly at that point, and would put the crew in the view of the hidden Rebs. The crew would start to argue loudly about the need to change the insulator, and then argue about whether the pole was safe to climb or not. Hopefully the Reb guards and the telegrapher would be distracted, giving the bridge guards a chance to get close, undetected. Purcell would slip up on the telegrapher from the side. Murphy's crew would be armed with the Spencers hidden in the wagon. Should the Rebs make a break for the pike, the crew could stop them.

The next day the two wagons left Brandy Station just as it began to get light. The telegraph construction crew was a few minutes in the lead. They turned off towards the ford and the guard's springwagon proceeded on towards the bridge. At the ford, Purcell exited the wagon just as it cleared the water. He then crawled over the riverbank and into the weeds and grass. Once inside the tall weed cover, he rose to his feet and crouched there waiting for the crew to start raising a ruckus. He heard Smith say,

"That insulator is not cracked. I am not going to climb that pole."

Murphy said, "It is, too. Now get your skinny young butt up that pole."

Bean chimed in, "The pole don't even look safe to climb."

Purcell was only a few feet away when the tapper turned and looked at him. He had a look of disbelief and then, complete horror on his young face. Purcell shoved the muzzle of the Henry against his chest. "Don't say a thing. Don't even move. I will shoot you in the blink of an eye," Purcell whispered.

The Reb nodded and froze in place. Purcell looked for a weapon and did not see one. To his amazement the boy was wearing leg shackles. They sat staring at each other for several minutes. Then he heard Bean shout, "They got them!"

"Stand up," Purcell ordered. He arose and helped the prisoner to his feet.

Bean had put his climbing hooks on and climbed the pole to gain a vantage point. "The soldiers and their prisoners are coming your direction, Shenandoah!" Bean shouted.

Purcell waved his arm in acknowledgment. "Okay fellow, walk towards the pike carefully."

"I don't think I can. I have been sitting there since before daylight yesterday."

"Here, move slowly and lean on me. Have you had anything to eat?" he asked as the youngster shuffled along.

"No, they said they would bring me something. But, they didn't. Don't put me with them, they will kill me. Canter does not leave witnesses."

"Which one has the key to those leg irons?"

"Canter, the big guy. Be careful, he is mean. He killed the jailer at Staunton. That is where he got these irons. The guy on the pole called you Shenandoah. Are you the guy from near Cross Keys?"

"I could be. Why do you ask?" Purcell quizzed.

"Everybody was talking how you outfoxed Striker. I think they were all for you. Striker robbed everybody and they hated him for it. My dad said Striker and Canter are cut from the some cloth."

"Where are you from?" Purcell asked.

"I am from Staunton. My folks own a store there. I worked in the Southern Telegraph office. They come and got me last week and said I was going to ride with them. They stole the sounder from the office at the same time. They would not even let me control the horse I was riding. They led me along, clear up the valley. They chained me to a tree when we stopped at night. They were afraid I would run if they let me loose. Canter took the shackles and a pistol off the jailer they killed. Neither one of them knows Morse Code. The short one climbed the pole with a rope on his feet. He made the connection."

"What is your name?"

"Harvey Jennings. I am 15 years old," he added. Purcell decided against telling the youngster that he was scarcely five years older than the kid was. The short beard helped hide Purcell's youth. He would just leave it that way.

The two men from the run were brought out and seated on the ground to await the guard's wagon. The lieutenant ordered the corporal to place them in the leg irons as soon as the wagon with the irons arrived.

"Shenandoah, it went off without a hitch. They were watching your men. We were on them before they knew we were anywhere around," the lieutenant said proudly.

"Lets keep the kid separate. He is just 15 years old. They kidnapped him and forced him into this. The tall one has the key to these shackles on the boy," Purcell explained.

The corporal retrieved the key and took the shackles off the youngster.

"I will take the kid in for interrogation. He might have information we can use."

"I doubt it. We need to find a way to send him back home to his parents at Staunton," Purcell said. He turned to Bean, "Go ahead and take the tap down."

Everyone was watching Bean on the pole. Purcell turned in time to see the larger of the two prisoners eying him and reaching into his boot. Purcell shot him just as the pistol cleared the boot. There was complete silence and then the corporal of the guard swore.

"Didn't anybody check him for a hide gun?" the lieutenant scolded. Quickly the corporal searched the remaining Reb and the young telegrapher and found no weapons. Purcell picked up the dead man's pistol. It was another small frame cartridge revolver. A .32 caliber Pond.

"It was a suicide move. He was figuring on taking the lieutenant and I with him. We were standing close together, and he was looking right at me. Maybe he was making a desperate bid to get one of our sidearms or this repeating rifle," Purcell said. He turned to the telegrapher, "Something is not quite right here. Harvey, what was he searching for on the telegraph?"

"Train destinations, train schedules, and any information on what they were carrying," the young telegrapher replied.

"Money trains," Bean said.

"Exactly," agreed Purcell.

The guard wagon arrived. The prisoner was put in wrist shackles and leg irons from the wagon, and loaded on it. The extra two soldiers rode the captured horses. Harvey rode his own horse without being led this time. The dead man was loaded on the construction wagon and covered with a wagon sheet. The day guards were dropped off at the railroad a short distance from the bridge. The wagons made their way back to Brandy Station.

At Brandy Station, the prisoners were brought into the command post. Purcell requested that the lieutenant let him take the boy over to Granger's and feed him. The lieutenant gave his permission. He asked, "Why do the telegraph people use those young kids to operate the message service?"

"It is simple. Youngsters learn the Morse Code easier than an older person. I was sending and receiving when I was a year younger than this boy. It has something to do with an inquisitive, uncluttered mind," Purcell explained.

Mae was on duty at the tavern, and she immediately fixed Harvey up with a plate of food. As Purcell paid Mae for the meal he asked if she had heard from their friend. Mae did not think Helen was home yet.

Granger came in from outside. "Well, Shenandoah, I hear you shot another man this morning."

"It was not my choice," Purcell answered.

The youngster sprang to Purcell's defense. "He was a bad one. He had even talked about robbing this place and the general store before he left town. Shenandoah didn't have a choice, Canter pulled a hide gun. I was there, I saw it."

"Okay, okay, enough," Granger laughed. "I don't know what it is about you, Shenandoah. Some people want to shoot you and some want to fight for you." Granger looked at Mae as he made the statement.

Purcell got the feeling that he had been discussed before.

Upon returning to the command post, Purcell heard some interesting facts from Lieutenant James. "Boyce, the remaining prisoner, did not want to talk at first. The corporal stayed with him while I went over to the guard house, and asked some Confederate prisoners for a volunteer burial detail. We have about a dozen waiting for parole. They took the oath not to return to the battlefield. They are not a bad lot. I got a burial detail, and when they went to unload the dead guy two of them identified him.

"He was a disgraced Partisan Ranger, the Rebs had tried him and sentenced him to hang for raping a woman and killing her family. He escaped before they could hang him. Boyce was in the same jail and escaped with him. They hatched the plot to kidnap a telegrapher, and get the inside information on bank and payroll shipments on the Federal side of the lines. There is not much money floating around on the Confederate side. Jones had been here during the battle for Rappahannock Station in '63. So he knew his way around."

His name was Jess Jones and he was going by the name of Canter. There are wanted posters on him. He was probably afraid Boyce would turn on him. When I confronted Boyce, he said that Jones knew he would be placed in irons and he knew we would find the jailer's pistol in his boot. So he took a chance before they put the irons on, and lost."

"Boyce is afraid you might shoot him, too. So he is talking up a storm."

"Why is he afraid I will shoot him?" Purcell asked.

"I think the corporal was working on him a little... You know, you shot the other guy right between the eyes."

Ignoring the remark, Purcell asked, "What are we going to do with Harvey Jennings?"

"I don't know. I will interview him tomorrow. After that, I will ask my superior officers. In the meantime, I will keep him away from Boyce and let

165

him bunk in the bridge guard's building. Boyce admitted they planned to kill Jennings when they had their information," the lieutenant added.

Chapter 11

Purcell went back to the telegraph office, and reported to McCorkle. He related how the operation went. "They forced the boy to go with them, and they stole the sounder and some wire. The sounder was an old large rascal that put a drain on the line. If it had not been for that we would not have detected it," Purcell explained.

McCorkle wanted to know where the prisoners were. Purcell solemnly explained that one was dead. "He pulled a gun from his boot. I had no other choice."

"Well, I would have shot him if I had been in your shoes," McCorkle admitted. "Shenandoah, if you ever hesitate in a situation like that, they will shoot you. So quit second guessing yourself."

"I know, I learned that lesson the hard way, and you are the second person to tell me that... What are we going to do with the kid?"

"I reckon he is the Army's problem," McCorkle argued.

"His family needs to know he is alive, and in safe hands."

"Oh, alright. I will talk to somebody," McCorkle conceded.

"I am sorry, McCorkle. I know what it is like to be broke and a long ways from home or friends... so I worry."

Purcell went back to the lieutenant's headquarters. He did not know quite what his plan was going to be. He did know that he might need a horse for the kid. He asked for the best horse of the three, which happened to be the one Jones was riding. The lieutenant was not sure he could do that.

"The boy needs to go home, and it may be that his only route back is through the Shenandoah. The way he came. They brought him here horseback. The kid would have a claim against Jones' belongings, if anybody has. I am alive today because I had a good horse under me," Purcell reminded him.

The lieutenant finally gave in and wrote a release. Purcell went down to the military pen yard, and obtained the horse and saddle. He took the roan gelding over to the telegraph yard and turned him in with the others.

That night he lay in his bunk, and mulled over what he might do to help the young Harvey Jennings. The Virginia Central Railroad was still virtually under control of the Confederacy from Culpeper south. There was no train traffic on the railroad north of Gordsville. If Jennings could get through the lines to Charlottesville and board a Staunton-bound train, he would be home if he could get through the fifty or so miles to Charlottesville. He could get shot as a spy, by either side, or conscripted into the Confederate army. If Sheridan or Hunter made a run at Staunton or Waynesboro, Jennings would be caught in the middle. Purcell decided that he had better give that up. He could not leave his job to take the boy back home, and the risk would be large if he did. He would wait and see what McCorkle came up with.

The next morning McCorkle went over some new plans to inspect and inventory telegraph lines in the district. Purcell was instructed to take a second man with him and inspect the the line from Rappahannock Junction to Manassas, Centerville, and Bullrun. He quite possibly would go on through the mountains, to Strasburg if it was in Federal hands. Mt. Jackson was out of the question.

"I want you to take a man with you to cover your back and assist. You can pick one of the construction crew, except Murphy. I need him here. I want you to inspect each telegraph station, check the equipment, and observe the operator. Make notes and I will need a written report with recommendations when you return. Take a couple days to get ready, and study the construction sketches. I notice that I now have another strange horse in my lot," McCorkle added.

"I convinced the lieutenant to let me have one of the captured horses for the young telegrapher," Purcell said. "He may need one to go home on. You can take its feed out of my wages, until we know what to do about the kid."

"We end up using your horses a lot. I am not going to charge you for the keep as long as we are using them. I notice the gray and the roan are well matched in size and body conformation. If they are harness broke, we will use them as a spare light team around the yard. Let's go eat breakfast," McCorkle said.

They stopped at the telegraph office on their way to breakfast and Williams handed Purcell a telegram. "Some guy sent you a telegram and just signed it with his initials. I hope you can figure it out," Williams said.

Purcell read the form. It was addressed to Stephen Purcell, Brandy Station, Virginia. The message read: "Shenandoah, I am home with my family. Many thanks. H.M."

At breakfast, McCorkle asked him which man he would choose to accompany him on the inspection trip. "If we expect a firefight, Bean is the man," Purcell said. "He is cool headed, and does his best work under pressure. Smith and Farley are both sharp and interested as well as personable. Smith has experience. Farley needs exposure, but he always comes through," Purcell declared. "So I guess I will take Farley."

"Good choice. Hey, looks like Granger has another big-eyed girl to replace the sharp-tongued gal. She don't move around as fast as the other one. She isn't carrying the extra load, either. By the way, I assume she made it home alright?"

"I assume she did, also," Purcell replied.

"You are not going to save up any money if you keep doing things like that," McCorkle scolded.

"It was the dead Reb's money. It did not feel good in my pocket. Are there any secrets in this little town?" Purcell answered.

McCorkle did not answer the question. He just smiled. He was not about to tell Purcell that he was in the office late the evening before, when the telegram came in.

"When you get to Warrenton Junction, follow the branch line off to the railroad. Stop there at the railroad depot. The line to Warrenton is disconnected. I imagine most of the wire has been stolen, anyway. I would like to keep the line on, but it would just be asking for trouble. They have fought back and forth over that town, and it has changed hands so many times that the churches have all been turned into hospitals. There are sick and wounded men from both sides over there. The town sure needs a telegraph, but it would virtually give the Confederacy their own private eavesdropping line. Mosby spends a lot of time in the area. Basically that is a large part of the problem."

As they left the tavern Purcell asked, "May I take time to check on the telegraph kid while I am in this end of town?"

"Sure. Stop by the office, and pick up a folder of sketch paper and a pencil or two. Then you can go up to the pens and talk to Farley about the assignment. You will need to pack bedrolls but you should be able to find lodging and meals most everywhere you are going. I will checkout traveling money for you. We will need to discuss the project some more."

Purcell went to the command post and found Jennings busy sweeping the floor. "Well I see they put you to work."

"Yeah, I always swept the floors at the Southern Telegraph Company office. I wonder who has been doing it since I have been gone. I hear you got an extra horse for me. Are we going back?" Jennings asked.

"Not for a while. There are a lot of bad things happening in the Shenandoah Valley right now. You cannot go back just yet. We need to get word to your parents that you are okay. Do you have any friends or family in Tennessee or Kentucky? It seems that the Confederates let mail come into southern Virginia from that direction sometimes. At least it happened a few times last year."

"I have an aunt and uncle, in Lexington, Kentucky," Jennings answered.

"Good, that is a place to start. Write to them and let them know you are okay. Ask them to get word to your parents if they can. It may or may not work. Talk to the people over at the Sanitary Commission, also. I have heard that they can get mail on Truce Flag Ships and blockade runners. Don't tell the family anything except that you are not hurt, and have escaped your captors. You can tell them that you are at Brandy Station, in good hands... The letter may be opened, and read by either side."

Back at the telegraph office, McCorkle had some new information. The Federal troops had control of Warrenton, and wanted the line and the railroad restored. That line would be the inspection team's first duty, and then they could finish the other line review. Purcell and Farley were to list what was needed, and then Murphy's crew would rebuild the line.

The rest of the afternoon was spent reviewing existing line drawings. Purcell could see some problems already in the original construction and pointed them out to McCorkle. The poles were set across country, and could not be reached easily. Being out of site from the pike made for much easier tampering. The experience in the overgrown field made him much more aware of fire problems. He advocated putting the lines alongside the pikes or railroads.

McCorkle explained that they were set that way to go the shortest distance and use less materials. He noted that the rural wagon roads usually twist and turn. Every turn in a telegraph line would require a anchor and brace wire. Most would require two. One going in each direction opposite the line turned. Heavier, larger glass insulators would be required.

After Purcell left to inform Farley of their new assignment, McCorkle leaned back in his chair and thought about Purcell. He was a thinking man and he was smart, but things there were different than in New York City. Young Purcell would learn much in the months to come.

Farley had been cleaning horse stalls all day. A chore that the newest employee on the construction crew usually drew when they had a light day. He was glad for a chance to go with Purcell.

The next morning they made their travel plans. Purcell would ride Colonel Ben, and Farley would ride the gentle black horse. They checked out a Spencer carbine for Farley. They took a single bit hand axe to sound the poles and cut vines with. A set of climbing hooks and wire pliers went into the leather carry roll that Farley would attach behind his saddle. A bed roll and rubberized poncho for each would complete the extra gear. Purcell would carry the dispatch case and telescope wrapped in an extra poncho. It would be difficult to work in the rain. If it started raining they would seek a place to shelter and wait it out.

Purcell would check the line out, and oversee the installation of new equipment at the railroad de-pot at Warrenton. New batteries and equipment would be needed as the former batteries and sending equipment had went south during an earlier occupation of Confederate troops. All this would depend on the condition of the line between Warrenton and the railroad junction. They would know before long.

As Purcell reviewed plans with McCorkle, the supervisor mentioned the high number of Confederate wounded still in the makeshift hospital in Warrenton. As they talked, an idea came to Purcell.

When he left the telegraph office, he rode on over to the lieutenant's office, and found the youngster from Staunton sitting behind the orderly's desk. "Today is my 16th birthday, so they are letting me sit behind the private's desk and pretend I am an orderly," Harvey crowed.

"Well orderly, I would like for you to write a letter to your folks. Address this envelope to them. I understand that there are many Confederate wounded at Warrenton. If we are lucky one of them might be going home and deliver it for you."

The lieutenant stepped through his office doorway. "Purcell you are always thinking. That is a great idea." He turned to Harvey, "Do not tell them you are a Federal orderly for a day. They may not like that."

Purcell took the letter and stowed it with his other paperwork. As he rode back across town he marveled at the kid's exuberance at being orderly for a day. Harvey was lucky he had fallen among friends on his birthday.

Purcell recalled that he had spent his 20th birthday up in the mountains running for his life. He held a deep hatred for the man named Striker. It just would not go away. Purcell intended to kill that man.

The next morning, Purcell and Farley rode out of town following the line in a northeasterly direction. Its close proximity to Brandy Station had ensured that it was in good repair. They inventoried one bad pole and two cracked insulators. Near the town of Warrenton Junction they came upon an anchor wire that a farmer's cattle had rubbed loose. Later, Purcell would make a memo advising that a reinforced short rail fence should be placed around the anchor and attached wire to fence the cattle away from it. He was certain that was the cause of the occasional garbled transmission received at Brandy Station and other locations. He couldn't blame the cows for scratching their backs. That just came natural for them.

They rode into Warrenton Junction just before dark. A local tavern had rooms so they put up for the night, stabling the horses at the livery next door. They secured the rifles and equipment in their room and went to supper.

They ordered their meal and Purcell surveyed the room. It looked like any other tavern crowd. A few sipping on mugs of ale, several were eating, and others just sitting silently. Purcell realized they were watching an obviously drunk Union army captain sitting at the end of the bar. It was easy to see the bar patrons' distaste for him. He was trying to engage the tavern keeper in conversation.

After awhile the Union captain got up and approached Purcell and Farley's table. He challenged them, saying they looked like Confederate spies. They ignored him and continued eating. The officer demanded to see identification. Purcell pulled the letter that McCorkle had written stating who he was and what his business was. He held the letter out to the man. "I am not looking at any damn made-up letter. I am going to take you into custody," the drunk man stated loudly.

He reached for his sidearm, fumbling with the holster. As he jerked the gun clear of the holster, Purcell came down hard on the man's wrist with his fist. The gun bounced along the floor. Purcell yanked his Colt, and shoved the barrel into the man's anatomy a few inches below his belt. "Move or even blink an eye and you are going to be missing a very important part of your person. Farley, hand him the letter. Now take the letter, and read it out loud." Purcell grabbed the officer's belt with his left hand, and jerked him hard against the revolver barrel. "Read it," he commanded, and cocked the gun.

The officer grabbed the letter and stumbled through it, slurring some of the words. Purcell released him, and he lurched for the door. In a split second Purcell realized the drunk had kept the letter. He threw his chair along the floor, and knocked the drunk's feet out from under him. He went down just before he reached the door. The letter went flying through the air. The drunk came up, like a cat, with a knife in his hand.

Purcell drew his revolver and cocked it again. "I don't think you want to do this drunk or sober," Purcell warned. The drunk reached back with his free hand and turned the latch knob. He slowly backed through the door. Once outside, the silent onlookers heard him run across the board floor of the porch. He was heading in the direction of the livery stable.

Purcell picked the pistol off the floor and handed it to the tavern keeper. "Give it to him when he comes back sober."

"Hasn't been sober for two days," the man said. "And, I have not been selling it to him. He has a jug some wheres else. He came in here drunk yesterday evening and came back again tonight," the tavern keeper was quick to add.

Purcell retrieved the letter from the floor and went back to his meal. Two men approached the table. "Mister, we are glad to see someone take that drunk Union blue coat down."

"I would rather that had not happened, but when he pulled his gun, I had no choice," Purcell explained.

"He was lucky. The last man that pulled a gun on Shenandoah, got a bullet between the eyes," Farley related, matter-of-fact like.

Purcell wished Farley had not said that.

Suddenly, Purcell had that strange feeling that something was not right. He remembered Adams had called his attention to a telegraph that came through from the Pinkerton agency. It had lain in the office for a couple of days before a Pinkerton detective had came through and picked it up. Some confidence men had stolen an officer's uniforms, side arm, and personal effects from a railroad luggage cart in Alexandria. The Pinkerton agency was under contract to do intelligence gathering and detective work for the government. Therefore, they had put out the word on the officer's stolen uniforms.

Rising from his chair, Purcell asked, "Does anybody know who he is?" Everyone, including the tavern keeper, indicated they did not. "Gentlemen, be advised that man was not drunk, and he is not a Union soldier. He was looking for someone to rob. A bulletin on the stolen Union uniforms came over the telegraph. He was trying to get us outside before we made him."

Turning to the tavern keeper, Purcell asked for the man's pistol to be returned. He checked the cylinder and found all six holes charged and capped. He removed one cap and rolled that empty nipple under the hammer. He handed the gun to Farley. He set his Colt at half cock, rolled the empty chamber back up, and let the hammer down. "We are going to check the horses. We could be walking into something. The livery stable attendant had a shotgun sitting in the corner behind his bunk in a box stall. That impostor ran across the front in the direction of the livery stable. He may have armed himself with the shotgun."

A tall, large man rose out of his chair and said, "I will go with you."

Purcell hesitated. The tavern keeper said, "He is alright. He is the constable. And mister, I am sorry, that bird asked me who you were. I told him you were telegraph people. I reckon I put the onus on you."

The constable pulled a badge out of his pocket and pinned it on his shirt. He produced a Colt from somewhere on his person.

"He will be waiting in the shadows between the horse barn and this building. There is an attendant and horses in the livery building. We don't want to fire into that building," the constable said.

"I agree. Let me go out and to the left so he will need to step out in the moonlight to follow me, or shoot at me. Tavern keeper, blow the lamp out at the window."

As soon as the light was out, Purcell said, "Farley, be ready to shoot in case he comes through the open door. Stay in here... Constable, I hope you can use that Colt."

"Well enough," the man replied.

Purcell stepped through the door, and flattened himself against the left wall. The Constable moved to the right towards the livery in the same manner. Purcell kept his eyes toward the livery stable as he sidled along the wall. When he reached the end of the wall he stepped out of the shadows, and into the moonlight.

A pistol barked to his left. Splinters from the porch post showered him. Purcell realized there was another shooter on his side of the building. Purcell dropped off the porch, landing on his knees. The assailant in the dark fired and missed again. Purcell returned fire, aiming slightly below where the muzzle flash had been. The gun went off again as the shooter fell face-first into the moonlit street.

Purcell heard the constable shoot two quick shots near the livery stable. Simultaneously, Farley threw himself out the door, landing flat on his stomach on the porch floor. He pointed the revolver and fired three deliberate shots towards the street. A man with a rifle fell to the ground across the street. Farley slowly stood up.

The constable broke the silence. "It worked. The guy you chased out of the tavern was in the shadow of the livery. He stepped out to shoot you in the back, but I got him. Stranger, are you okay?"

"Yes, I am fine," Purcell answered. "Farley, how about you?"

"I am sorry. I left my post, Shenandoah. I did not think you saw that one across the street," Farley said.

"I did not see him. Thanks. Are you okay?"

"Yes."

"What do we have, three of them down?" the constable asked.

"I hope that was all of them. Farley, ask that tavern man to bring a lantern out here," Purcell said.

"I know where they hang the one in the livery," the constable said, and turned toward the livery. He picked up the shotgun, and kicked the downed man, just for good measure. Purcell checked on the one he shot. He was still breathing. Purcell removed his pistol, and checked for other sidearms. That one also wore an ill-fitting Union captain's uniform. Purcell started toward the livery door and heard the constable swear.

Purcell walked over to where the constable stood holding the lantern. "He killed him in his bed," the constable said. "The bastard stabbed the poor kid with the same damned knife he pulled on you. Just to get to the shotgun."

"If I would have figured it out I would have shot him then... The one I did shoot, on the left is still alive," Purcell added.

They walked across the street to check the third man. Farley joined them. "You did good. Three bullets out of three in him, with a strange gun," the constable said.

"Yes. I had to shoot him three times. He just would not let go of the rifle," Farley replied.

Several of the tavern customers walked over to where the body was. "They are all strangers," the constable said. "Smithers, go get the undertaker. Jonesy, go get the doc for the wounded fellow, and then stop by the judge's house and tell him I need a coroner's jury first thing in the morning. Tell him two, maybe three dead strangers, and Mikey at the livery. Yeah, I know he was a damn good kid. Somebody go pull the blanket up over him, and stay there 'til the undertaker gets here. Tell the undertaker that I said to tend to Mikey first. The rest of you hang around. We are going to need help moving these bodies.

"I have some questions for you, Mr. Purcell. Burt, you watch this body. Andy, you watch the one over there. He is still alive. Don't let anyone take anything. The guns are part of the coroner's inquest. The judge will act as coroner. You can let the dogs eat on the one over by the livery for all I care."

As Purcell watched and listened, he was gaining a new respect for small town constables. They went into the tavern and sat down at a table. "Now tell me why they were interested in you? You might also explain why you keep your sidearm hidden under your jacket?"

"I figure that the one in here was looking for some travelers to rob. The drunk act and the uniform was a good cover. When the barkeep told him that we were telegraph employees he began to worry because there were telegrams going through on the stolen uniforms. When I messed up his "arrest," he figured I would come after him to get the letter back. The other two would have moved in. They were standing watch. If they had disarmed us, they would have took us to the edge of town and shot us. He knew we might put it together, and I did, but it was too late for that kid in the livery. As far as my pistol, I have a bullet wound at the top of my hip and can not wear a weighted belt on it."

"Now," Purcell said. "I have a question for you. How come you did not step in to help him arrest us? Or at least, identify yourself?"

"You all should know that around here we don't have much respect for blue coats. And, I don't flash the badge unless I need to... I will need both pistols you took off them. By the way, that was a couple of fancy moves you made on him. I just wish you would have shot him. I wish I would have shot him before I did.

"Go to bed and get some rest, I will handle it from here on. Don't leave. You will need to stay for the coroner's inquest tomorrow morning. Shouldn't take long. I must go get my wife now, to go with me to tell that kid's mother that her only son is dead. She lost her husband during the Cedar Mountain fight."

"If you find identification on those men, I can telegraph it to the Pinkerton office in Alexandria tomorrow," Purcell offered.

The constable nodded agreement.

They went to their room and attempted to sleep. From his bunk, Farley broke the silence. "It was not a strange gun. It is a Remington Army. My father has one just like it. I have shot it at targets many times. It has a post type front sight that sticks up. That is why it hung up in his holster. If he would have pulled the gun straight up, it would have came out easier."

"It gave me the time I needed to react. Try to get some sleep. We have a lot ahead of us tomorrow," Purcell said. "Thanks again for covering my back."

Chapter 12

Constable David Daniels marveled at the strength of Charlotte Reed. How much more could the poor woman take? She had lost her husband to the war, and now her son to a common criminal. The shotgun belonged to the livery stable owner and not the kid. The boy would probably have given it up willingly, but he would have alerted the constable. So the murdering pile of manure killed him for it.

The boy's father and Daniels were best friends. They had joined the Confederate Army together and fought several battles without a scratch.

Then on Cedar Mountain his friend was killed, and Daniels was wounded and captured.

At the Federal prison camp, Daniels was offered the chance for parole if he would take the oath not to bear arms against the Union. He was sick. He was seeing wounded and sick men dying all around him. He was sure that he was going to die. So he took the oath, just to see home again. He underestimated the power and care of a loving wife and good friends. His wounds began to heal. The cough and labored breathing slowly went away. He had been town constable when he left to go to war. They re-elected him as soon as his health would allow him to work again.

Constable Daniels had wanted to step in and help Purcell, but he knew he had to give Union soldiers, especially officers, a wide berth. All the locals in the room knew that. When the scoundrel ran towards the livery, Daniels knew he had to stand up and be counted. It would always haunt him that he did not act sooner.

Farley had twice called the man named Purcell the nickname Shenandoah. Yet, Purcell was working for the Federally controlled telegraph system. It occurred to Daniels that Purcell probably had a past, too.

Daniels left his wife to stay with the grieving Mrs. Reed until the woman's daughter could get there to be with her. He returned to the site of the gun-fight, and was told that the doctor wanted him to come to the wounded holdup man. The man had been moved to the feed store. The onlookers had laid out sacks of grain to make a bed and placed a saddle blanket over him.

"Not much of a bed to go out on," Daniels thought to himself.

The doctor told him that the man knew he was dying and wanted to make a confession. The man verified that the uniforms, were in fact, stolen. That the trio of robbers had used them to gain the trust of several robbery victims in Washington. But, they had not been as successful in Virginia. They were out of money and desperate when they came up with the drunk officer act. The rest of the story was much as Shenandoah, the telegraph man, had sup-posed.

The next morning, the village justice of the peace, acting as coroner, called a meeting to order in a corner of the tavern dining room. The breakfast customers listened in. A clerk from the general store wrote down the statements of each person involved, as well as each onlooker from the tavern. The wit-nessed confession of the dying robber was submitted by the constable.

The acting coroner first ruled that young Mikey Reed died at the hand of one "John Doe," real name unknown. The justice of the peace then ruled a justified homicide for each of the three dead robbers. The justice, for the record, commended Constable Daniels and his duly drafted and commissioned deputies, Purcell and Farley, for a job well done.

It was almost noon before Purcell and Farley started up the line towards the railroad and the Warrenton spur. Purcell recorded another loose anchor and a bad pole. They took time to remove a couple of vines. It was close to the end of the day when they arrived at the telegraph and train station. Purcell went inside to identify himself and Farley.

"Well, you must have got a late start. McCorkle's telegram said you would be here about noon," the telegraph operator said.

Purcell ignored the inquisitive operator. "I want to check the battery and the rest of the office equipment. Farley, have you ever looked inside a battery? We are going to open the switch and take you offline for a few minutes," he told the operator.

Purcell removed the top, and surveyed the plates and the acid level. "Acid level looks good here. You never want to spill even a drop of the liquid on you. It is caustic. It is made by suspending a bag of vitriol in the water to create an acid that reacts with the copper and zinc plates. An electric current is produced between them."

"What is vitriol?" Farley asked.

"I do not know the exact chemical composition, but it is basically powdered sulphates," Purcell explained.

"Hey, you know a lot about the telegraph business for a gunfighter," the operator remarked.

Purcell frowned, and asked, "Why do you think that?"

"It's been all over the wire today. All about a gang of thieves and murderers made the mistake of accosting a couple of gun-toting telegraph men and a tough small town constable." He continued, "Pinkerton is saying that those guys have killed several people. I reckon you fellows were lucky."

"I guess we were at that," Purcell dismissed the subject. "Where can we find lodging?"

"Widow Tompkins has a boarding house down the road 'bout a quarter mile. Calls it Tompkin's Inn. She feeds good. She's nice to look at. She don't allow swearing or misconduct at her table. She says grace at every meal, and prays for our boys to come home safely. When she says our boys, she ain't talkin' about Union boys. Don't say anything out of the way to her or her help, or you and your duffel will wake up out in the cold... She's a war widow, as are most of the widows around here," he added.

"Whew, sounds like hell on wagon wheels," Farley commented.

"Nope, and it will be the cleanest, best bed you ever slept in," the operator replied.

They arrived at a large two story frame house with a single story porch around three sides. The lady of the house met them at the door and sized them up. "Are you looking for supper, or meals and a room for the night?

"We are wanting a room, supper, and breakfast," Farley answered.

"The barn for your horses is at the end of the lane. There is a negro man at the door of the alley between the stalls. You must give him one dollar to look to your horses and gear. That money is for him. The hay and grain for the horses comes with the cost of your room. There is a sink facility for gentlemen to the left of the woodshed near the back of the yard. There is a washroom and bathhouse at the lean-to on the side of the summer kitchen. Hot water is on the stove at all times. Clean towels are folded on a shelf on the west wall. You may wash up and come to supper at six-thirty. The dining room is at the rear of the house. You will be seated promptly at the appointed time. I see you have rifles on your saddles. You may leave them with the man at the barn. He has a locker there and they will be secure. I allow no firearms or smoking in the house. You will pay me two dollars and fifty cents each before you leave in the morning.

Broken down, that is a dollar-fifty for the room and fifty cents for each meal, per man. I suggest you leave a two-bit piece in the room when you leave, if you want the maid to remember you in good humor. You will not receive your horses in the morning until you have paid me. Better hurry along now or you will be late for supper."

Supper went just as the telegraph operator said it would be. Not overly bountiful but all you needed to eat. The guests included a man and his wife, a salesman, a minister, and Purcell and Farley.

After supper they retired to the sitting room. The hostess played the piano while the guests were served a glass of apple brandy. The story of her inn came together in pieces.

Her husband, a Confederate colonel, was killed in the Battle of Bull Run. Facing difficult times, she had called a meeting of the farm hands and the servants. They would continue operating the plantation. Together they arrived at the idea of making an inn of the large house to generate cash to supplement the farm crops and produce. She gave the servants the opportunity to leave. Not a one left, citing that the plantation was their home, too. The plan was working. Over the last two years she had hosted many travelers, including Confederate and Federal officers. Her strictly all-business manner served her well.

After they retired, Purcell and Farley agreed it was a pleasant place to stay. A bit expensive, but tomorrow they could be sleeping in their bedroll on the ground. As he settled back in the comfortable bed, Purcell realized he had not slept much the night before. The lady had said there would be a wakeup bell at six a.m. and breakfast was served at seven.

As they were paying the bill and getting ready to leave, Purcell decided he would try to enlist her help with the Jennings' letter. "Mrs. Tompkins, I have a problem that I think you might be able to help me with. May we talk privately?"

"Well, you have already paid your money. So it must be a proposition. I have occasionally been propositioned in the evening, but this is the first time for a morning try. Shame on you. I am old enough to be your mother," she smiled.

He stammered, "Madam, I assure you it is not a proposition..." Then he realized she was making fun of him. Maybe even flirting with him. It was for sure the dragon lady was delighting in embarrassing him. He smiled back.

"Come to the kitchen," she said. He followed her there. She stopped, and stood by a chair at the table. "Well," she said. "A gentlemen seats a lady."

Quickly, he rushed to hold her chair for her. He returned to the other side and sat opposite her. "I am almost disappointed. Whatever is it, Shenandoah? I heard them call you that. I don't have a lot of time."

He explained the Harvey Jennings story, and the need to get a letter through to the Jennings boy's parents at Staunton. "I had the idea, that while I was working at Warrenton that I might get someone in the Confederate Hospital to carry it back past the lines."

"And, you want me to give you a contact."

"Yes, should you know someone."

She was silent for a long time. He thought she was going to refuse. She made eye contact with him, and after a pause, she asked, "Do you have a piece of paper and a pencil?"

He handed her a piece of the sketching paper from his pocket. She took it and wrote, "Alisha Stewart, Nurse, CSA, at the first brick church on your left as you go into town." She handed the paper back to him. "Nurse Stewart might be able to help you. You just might get lucky."

He got up and approached her as if to again hold her chair. When she turned toward him he placed his hand under her chin, and turned her face up. "Thank you! You are a nice person, and one beautiful lady." He gave her a big kiss on the mouth.

"I think I just got lucky! You better go young man."

She sat at the table smiling for a long time after he had left. She finally arose, went to her library, and obtained a sheet of paper and an envelope at the writing desk. She sat down and addressed the envelope to Alisha Stewart. The letter read:

A young man will be calling on you to ask the favor of your assistance. He is trying to get a letter through the lines to Staunton. His name is Stephen Purcell. He is from Cross Keys, and they call him Shenandoah. I have suggested that you might help him. He is handsome, intelligent, and polite for the most part. I must admit, he made this older woman's heart flutter. Help him if you can. If you are so inclined, give him a hug and a kiss, and say I sent it to him. Thanking you in advance.

Your friend,
Kathryn Tompkins.

Kathryn Tompkins told herself that she may have found the young man that could bring Alisha Stewart out of her lost romance funk. She sealed the envelope and called for a servant to deliver it.

The line inspection went well. Surprisingly, a large part of the wire was still there. Several poles needed to be changed and a few insulators replaced.

Railroad crews were busy repairing and re-placing damaged sections of the rail system. The crews were rebuilding burned bridges over some of the runs. At the depot, broken windows were being replaced. Roof repairs were underway. The tele-graph equipment was no longer there. The next morning he would ride back to the railroad junction and wire a materials report to McCorkle.

Purcell and Farley rode into the town, and turned up the street to the Warren Green Hotel. The hotel was a large building with a porch running across the front with stairs up to the center of the porch. The room and board prices were the same as at Mrs. Tompkin's inn. The accommodations were not as nice, and the proprietor did not play the piano after supper.

The next morning, Purcell returned to the railroad junction and wired the list of materials and a report to McCorkle. He stayed around the depot waiting for a return wire. The talkative agent in-quired about his stay at the Tompkin's Inn. "Ain't she a looker?"

"Yep, she plays a nice piano, too." Purcell turned and walked over to the window.

The receiver began to click. The message came back. The materials would be loaded and on the way, by the next morning. McCorkle was sending Smith, Bean, and two other construction men. He had sent Murphy to Fredericksburg to oversee crews and the distribution of the wire and supplies shipped there by boat. Purcell was charged with supervision of the reconstruction of the Warrenton line and placing it in use once again. A newly-trained telegrapher would be sent in from Washington.

Purcell returned to Warrenton and assisted Farley in re-tensioning and installing new tie wires on the insulators at the depot building. He decided to contact the nurse the next morning while they were waiting for the supplies and crews to arrive.

Alisha Stewart watched the two men ride up to the rear entrance of the church. She stood in her own little box of a room. In normal times, it would have been a church cloak room. Now it was her refuge from the world of pain and suffering she had observed for two years. She had a cot, a chair, a small table for a desk, and one window. The window overlooked the rear churchyard.

She wondered why the horsemen chose the back entrance. The one riding the large fancy horse dismounted and took off his buckskin jacket. He removed a pistol and a holster from under his left arm.

He handed the gun to the second man along with the bridle reins. He put his jacket back on and started up the steps. He walked with an air of confidence. He had a neatly trimmed, short, dark beard. She knew that he must be the man called Shenandoah.

He entered the unlocked back door and started down the hall past her door when she opened it. "Mr. Purcell, I presume?" she called to his back.

He turned and nodded his head indicating that he was.

"Come in, I have been expecting you. Kathryn had a note delivered to me."

Purcell suddenly felt awkward. She was striking, even in the rumpled dress and stained apron. She had eyes that seemed like dark pools, raven hair, and a light complexion with a perfect face. The rest of her matched perfectly. He told himself that Nurse Stewart was the prettiest girl that he had ever seen. Stephen Purcell was suddenly both smitten and speechless.

"Yes, Mr. Purcell?" she said.

"I am sorry," he scrambled to recover. "I did not expect a nurse to be so young... and so pretty. Well," he stammered. "I sure messed that up."

She didn't smile. She didn't frown. She just said, "I am told that several times a day."

She stepped back and motioned him into the room. "Where is the letter you wanted sent up the valley? I hope it is not a private letter. I would like to read it. I am careful about what I am a part of. I am sorry I have only one chair. You may sit on the bed if you like."

"I can understand that you want to read the letter, and I will be happy to answer any questions you might have." He opened the envelope and handed the letter to her.

She read it, and looked over at him. He told her the story of how he found young Harvey Jennings in chains, and discovered the boy had been kidnapped.

Purcell said, "I have placed a dollar in the envelope in case some postage is needed on up the line."

"I think I can get it there. You are to be commended for doing this for the unfortunate boy. I am from the Staunton and Port Republic areas. That will help," she said rising from the chair. "Did Kathryn show you the letter she wrote to me?"

"No ma'am, she must have written it after I left the day before yesterday."

"You must have made quite an impression on her."

"She seems to be a remarkable woman," he replied.

"She told me to give you a hug and a kiss for her. In the two years I have known her, I have not seen or heard of her hugging and kissing anybody."

"I am sorry, I am sure it was just a figure of speech."

"There is no problem. I get my hand kissed and a marriage proposal at least twice a day."

"Thank you, and I don't doubt the marriage proposals one bit." He turned to go.

On an impulse, she reached out and caught his arm. She did not know why, but suddenly, Kathryn's suggestion made sense. "I just don't know how sane I am. I was about to pass up a hug from a vertical man."

She gave him a peck on the cheek, and hugged him.

He awkwardly hugged her back. He stammered out, "With all due respect ma'am, I will hug you anytime you want."

As they broke the embrace, she let her arm slip down, and her wrist touched the top of the hip bandage. She examined the bandage through his shirt. "Have you been wounded?"

"Yes, three times, to be exact."

"When?"

"About seven, maybe eight weeks ago. Somewhere around Thornton's Gap and Sperryville. The other two have practically healed. That one is finally healing."

"That is why you were carrying the pistol under your arm."

"You are the first person that has not asked me why I carried it that way. How did you know I carried a pistol?"

"I saw you take it off when you dismounted. Do all telegraph employees carry guns?"

"Yes ma'am, mostly anyhow. I would not have been able to rescue that boy if I had not been armed. We must carry arms to protect ourselves and the equipment."

"How old are you?" she asked.

"I am twenty, and I figure that is about how old you are, also."

They were interrupted by the ring of a hand-bell down the hall. "Hear that bell?" Alisha asked. "There is an emergency. I must go. I would like for you to call on me again, sometime. We can talk about our home area."

"Will I get another hug?" he teased.

"You just might," she replied coyly as she rushed out the door.

Purcell returned to Farley and the horses. He retrieved the Colt and holster, and mounted up.

"Well, will she help?"

"I think so."

"What did she look like?"

"One time, I heard Aunt Eppie describe a woman she had just met as being delightfully pretty in face and form. I could describe Nurse Stewart in that manner." He added, "Very much so."

Chapter 13

Kathryn Tompkins wondered if her attempt at playing cupid would work. Alisha Stewart had traveled north to work as a nurse at Warrenton so she could be close to her boyfriend. The day she arrived, he told her that his unit had been consolidated into another one, and they were going into Tennessee. That was the last she had heard of him. She was eighteen then, and that had been almost two years ago. That was too long to wait for a man to communicate. If he was alive she would have heard from him. A search by some of Kathryn's late husband's Confederate officer friends turned up no such person.

They thought that he may have been an impostor, using the uniform to impress the girls. Perhaps if he was a soldier, he had just lost interest. That was doubtful. Only a fool would lose interest in a girl like that.

Even though she had matured considerably, two years was too long for a girl that young to see the horrors she had seen day after day. She needed to get herself out of there and move on with her life. The telegraph crew supervisor called Shenandoah seemed like a good match. They were both spirited and smart. She was pretty, and he was handsome... Well, she told herself time would tell.

When the materials arrived, Purcell started the new crew with the pole wagon. They replaced poles ahead of Bean and Smith as they climbed poles and replaced broken insulators. Next came the wire splices and ties. Purcell and Farley installed the battery and sending/receiving equipment in the railroad depot. Purcell figured they would be through in three or four days.

A landowner challenged their right to have a line on his property. Purcell figured the landowner's rejection had more to do with the war than anything else. Purcell solved the problem by having that section of the line moved to the railroad right of way. The railroad agent was more then happy to facilitate the line. The agent knew the railroad would use the line as much or more than others. The line move added several days to the project.

Purcell could also see the possibilities. He recommended to McCorkle to construct independent crossings on the two largest runs and stay off the railroad bridges. All this took more time.

To attach the line to the bridges was an easy and flood-safe crossing, but not in time of conflict. When the bridge was blown or burned, the telegraph went with it. When this hateful war was over, the crossings could go back to the bridges.

McCorkle agreed, and sent the extra poles and anchor material to effect the separate crossings. Purcell had requested that McCorkle send pine or coal tar to coat the below ground portion of the crossing poles. McCorkle did not send it. It was in short supply due to the war. Purcell lamented the fact that the poles set in wet ground would be eaten away in a year or two by bugs and rot. He had observed and overheard discussions on that construction problem when he was at the telegraph office in New York City.

The days went by quickly, and near the end of the week McCorkle wired orders for them to take Sunday off. Purcell let the men off early Saturday afternoon. He had something he wanted to do.

On his way back into town he stopped at the church hospital to leave a note inviting Nurse Alisha to supper Sunday. He went in the front door this time. He asked an older woman at a makeshift desk near the front to give the note to Alisha.

"Would you like to talk to her yourself? I will get her." The woman did not give him time to say no, as she rushed off to get Alisha.

Alisha appeared and removed the stained apron as she made her way to the front. As before, she did not smile. "We can talk out in the vestibule," she said. They walked back into the entrance of the church.

"I apologize," Purcell said. "I am not very presentable. I intended to just leave a note inviting you to supper tomorrow evening. Would you consider that?"

"Please wait here. I will ask my supervisor if I may have tomorrow evening off." She turned and went back through the door.

Purcell clearly heard the woman at the desk say, "Girl, if you turn this one down, I am going to run out there and throw myself in front of his horse to keep him from leaving."

Nurse Alisha returned and said, "She gave me the whole weekend off beginning now. What did you have planned for this evening?"

"Nothing, just to take a bath and eat and sit around the hotel. But, we can do that together if you are available," he blurted out.

The girl that never smiled, burst out laughing. "I believe we should take separate baths, sir."

Purcell was glad his beard covered part of his red face. "I am sorry ma'am, I said that all wrong."

"I know. I was teasing you." She stepped forward quickly, and embraced him. She realized that all she needed was a small excuse. Propriety be hanged, this guy she wanted to know better. "We will need a horse with a sidesaddle, or a horse and carriage so I can keep my shoes and skirts out of the muddy street. They rent horses and buggies at the livery. Do you think you can get all that done in, say two hours?"

"You know I can," Purcell replied, and turned to leave.

"Just a minute," she said. She gave him a kiss on the cheek above his beard. "Thank you for coming back. I was not sure you would." Purcell left smiling.

He stopped at the livery. He arranged to rent a buggy and harness for Colonel Ben. Purcell reserved the buggy for that evening and Sunday. The horse had not been in harness since the potato patch, but Purcell had no worries about the big horse adjusting to a buggy.

At the hotel, he paid the attendant to fill one of the wooden tubs in the bathhouse with warm water. He scrubbed hard at several day's worth of sweat, dirt, and grime that had accumulated. He dried off and paid the attendant for a packet of scented powder. He had a clean pair of brown canvas pants, a blue shirt, and a black wool jacket he had bought at the general store. All of a sudden, he wished he had some better clothes.

He trimmed his short beard, and tidied up in general. He made a pass at cleaning up his boots. He wished he had brought a better pair of boots with him. Purcell was traveling light, but this was a special occasion. He had met girls at church and socials. He had never met one as pretty as this one. In fact, he had never met one that affected him like this one.

He went to the livery and found they had the Colonel hooked up to the buggy, ready to go. When he turned into the street the horse hit the fast moving trot, as he had been trained to do. The only thing missing was Eppie and Granville.

When he arrived at the church, he maneuvered the buggy so that the right side was against the boardwalk. He tied the horse and went in. The same woman was at the desk. She was all smiles as she said, "I will tell her you are here. Please have a chair."

Purcell looked around and took the lone chair across and back from the desk. He smiled to himself. That chair was not there two hours ago.

The lady returned, saying, "She will be ready in a few minutes. Tell me, did I hear her laugh today while you two were talking in the vestibule?"

"Yes, I said something awkward and funny. Her laughter sounds like music. Doesn't it?" he remarked.

"In all the time I have known her, that is the first time I have heard her laugh. I hope you keep saying awkward, funny things. That girl needs to laugh," the woman declared.

He looked around. It was a church turned hospital, with high ceilings, a choir loft, and stained glass windows. This church was a place of peace and hope, and now a place of pain and death. Then he realized it still would be a place of peace, hope, and solace for the men that were brought here.

Suddenly he began to hear whistles and murmurs. One voice called out, "Way to go, Nurse Stewart. Who is the lucky man?"

"I should have had you come to the other door," she said as she walked up to Purcell.

"Are you sure? You not only have made my day. It sounds as if you made the day brighter for others, too."

"And you say that you speak awkwardly," the desk person chimed in. "You two, enjoy your evening."

As he helped her into the buggy, he said, "You look fabulous. All in two hours! Your hair is just ... beautiful."

She laughed again. "Stop that! You embarrass me. You are lucky I washed my hair this morning or it would have taken longer than two hours."

He untied Ben and backed the buggy into the street. "Do you have a place that you would prefer to eat? The only place I know is the hotel, and it is pretty plain."

"Yes as a matter of fact I do. Do you see that tall church steeple over there? Turn left when you get to the next street over, and drive towards that church. At the bottom of the hill, before we get to the church, there will be a restaurant sign. Turn left again and we should be right there. I have eaten there with some of my sister nurses." She added, "It will be quieter there and there will be a better menu. It may be slightly higher-priced."

"That is alright. I am courting a pretty classy gal tonight."

"Oh, do you court many gals, Shenandoah?"

"Well I did it again. No, I have not really courted any girls. I guess, I must depend on you to help me get through the evening."

"You have kissed girls before. I would wager that."

"Yes," he admitted. "But, stealing a kiss or two in a dark corner at a barn dance is not exactly courting."

"I am sorry I have been teasing you. I promise I will behave, at least through supper."

Purcell realized she was teasing, but she was also trying to find out more about him. He began to worry what she would think when his "gunfighter" reputation surfaced.

Once out on the street, Colonel Ben hit his stride and away they went. "This is the same horse you were riding!" she exclaimed.

"Yes, he is an all around saddle and harness horse. He is a new breed called Kentucky Saddler. I owe my life to him. He has kept me out of harm's way."

They were seated at an out-of-the-way table. They ordered their meal, and turned immediately to inquiring of each other's background.

"Kathryn's note said you are from around Cross Keys? Incidentally, your letter is well on the way to Staunton. In fact, it may be there by now," Alisha informed him.

"How did you get it there that fast? he asked.

She replied, "My parents live in Staunton. Kathryn Tompkins knew that. That is why she sent you to me. I just put his letter in with mine. My parents probably know the Jennings boy's parents. At any rate, they will get it to his family. My grandparents lived at Port Republic. I have spent many happy hours there with them. They may know your family."

"How do you know Kathryn Tompkins?" he asked.

"She came to the hospital to help, during the Second Battle of Manassas. She was already a widow and still grieving. I was new, having been at the hospital just a few months. I marveled at her inner strength. We worked together for several months. Since starting her inn, she has not worked here. She keeps in contact."

"How long have you worked at the hospital?"

"I have been here two years."

"Are you a trained nurse?"

"Not really, I went to the Female Academy in Staunton, and had one year training with a doctor in Harrisburg before the war brought me here."

"Well, you are trained now," he offered.

"Enough about me. Let us talk about you," she said.

That was exactly what Purcell did not want to do. "There is really not much to talk about."

"How did you become a telegraph crew supervisor at such a young age?"

That gave Purcell a little room to work. He knew he would have to tell her the whole story, sometime, but not today. "I grew up in New York City. My father was a sea captain, my mother died early on, and of course he could not take me with him. I ended up in a private boarding school, and then at a preparatory school. I think they intended to make a ship's captain out of me. However, I started working part time at a telegraph office.

"My father went down with his ship when I was fifteen years old. They located my mother's uncle, Granville Coldiron, near Cross Keys and Port Republic. I was sent to live with him. I lived with them five years. People I have met since came up with the name Shenandoah. I have a basic knowledge of the technical and mechanical operation of the telegraph. That is where I am at. Part of my job is finding and clearing taps, and checking the line. On this project, the area supervisor has made me responsible for the construction crew."

"Where is your uncle's farm?"

"It was on the east side of the Shenandoah River, between the river and the Blue Ridge Mountains. Uncle Granville used to say we were in the morning shadow of the mountains. The place was on north of Cross Keys and Port Republic. We crossed the river at a ford. If the river was up, it was easier to go to Port Republic than to cross the river to Cross Keys. My aunt and uncle were both born and raised in the Cross Keys area."

Purcell and Alisha shared the experience of going to private schools. They talked about the funny things that happened. The pranks, and things that went on behind the professor's back. Purcell drove the buggy up and down the street a couple of times, then it was time to take her back.

"Drive around behind. The door will be locked, but I have a key."

He brought Ben to a halt, but did not get out.

"Aren't you going to help me out?"

"No. Not until you tell me if I can call on you, or take you to church tomorrow."

"I was just kidding anyway," she said. "So lets talk it over. What do you want to do? I do not think I want to go to church. Not yet. It would start tongues to wagging. I have been attending by myself for two years, you know. This congregation is meeting in homes and brush arbors. The church on the hill has overflow crowds."

"I have the buggy for tomorrow. Of course you would need to show me where to go. I am not acquainted with the area."

"I can prepare a picnic basket and we can go for a drive in the country, perhaps to the springs just west of town. The way this horse travels we would be there in less than a half hour. You may pick me up about ten o'clock. Well, now that we have that settled, I can leave," she giggled.

"Well, if you must," he replied.

"Well, maybe not just yet," she said, and moved over against him. "You really haven't courted much. Have you Stephen? May I call you Stephen? I don't want to call you Shenandoah. That is what the newspaper called you. I read all about it, you know."

"Where do I start?" he asked himself out loud. She was silent.

"First of all, no, honestly I have not courted at all. Second, yes you may call me by my given name, or any name you choose. Certainly you may call me Stephen. That is my real name. Now, what newspaper?"

"The Alexandria News. There was a big write-up last week on how Warrenton Junction, Constable Daniels, and Federal Telegraph employees, namely one 'Shenandoah' Purcell and a Mr. Farley, took on a trio of murderers and robbers in a desperate shootout on Warrenton Junction's main street, and won."

"I wanted to tell you sometime," Purcell sighed. "There have been other shootouts. I have taken lives, and you are saving lives. I was afraid you might not want to have anything to do with me."

She was silent for a moment. "It is the times we live in. I have no problem with what happened at Warrenton Junction. I have things that I am struggling with, but I will not tell you tonight. I will tell you that I have never felt any more comfortable with a man than I feel tonight. Let us walk to the door."

She unlocked the door, and turned. He kissed her good night. She hugged him tightly. Then she turned, and went quickly into the building.

Chapter 14

The next morning he drove around behind the church and she met him at the door with a picnic basket. He took it from her hand, and noted two corked wine bottles sticking up from the cover. "My," he said. "Are we going to have a picnic with two bottles of wine?!"

"That is lemonade, silly boy. It was Maggie's idea. We will use the yarn string to hang them in the spring. After about an hour they should be good and cold. Most of the springs around Fauquier County are sulfur springs, but this one, they say, is also very cold."

"Who is Maggie?"

"She is the head nurse, and my supervisor. She, among others, have been trying to find me a beau. She is delighted that the telegraph man is calling on me. They will be watching from the windows. So don't get too affectionate, and watch where you put your hands."

"What should I do, keep my hands in my pockets?"

"No, smart guy, take my hand, and steady me when I step up."

He set the basket under the seat from the back, and on top of the blanket that covered the Henry. He followed her directions, and they were soon out of town. The grade changed, and the Blue Ridge was visible once again in the far distance. She moved over against him, and put her hand on his arm. "I am sorry that I am so bossy. But, you said for me to help you through this courting thing."

"I suspect being a bit bossy comes with being a nurse. You have learned to take charge, and you have earned the right to be a bit bossy. I know I too, am sometimes a bit decisive on the job."

They came out of the timber from each side of the road. It was a perfect place for highwaymen to hide. Two with rifles pointed hung back and to the sides of the road. The four remaining ones approached. They wore gray uniforms with Confederate markings.

Purcell knew he could not put up a fight. He would die before he would risk harm to the girl.

"My, my, Cap'n would you look at that fancy horse?" one of the young ones crowed...

Alisha greeted the leader. "Hello, Captain McNeill."

The man she called Captain McNeill immediately removed his hat. "I apologize, I certainly did not recognize you under that bonnet, Miss Stewart."

"This is my friend Stephen Purcell. He is from my home area near Staunton," she said.

"Pleased to meet you, Mr. Purcell. We will be moving on." He waved his hand and the riders turned their mounts up the road.

McNeill hung back, turning his horse back toward the buggy. He said, "Mr. Purcell, any friend to Nurse Stewart or Dave Daniels is a friend of mine." He put the spurs to his horse and was gone.

"He has brought more than a few wounded men for us to work on," she explained.

"It sounds like he reads the newspapers, too," Purcell replied.

"Would you have let them take your horse?"

"I had already decided to let them take the horse rather than risk getting you hurt in a gun battle.

However, it would have been a mistake for them to take him and let me live," he said, matter-of-fact like.

"What would you have done if they had taken me?" she asked coyly.

"You mean, tried to take you," he replied.

They reached a pasture, and a grove of trees with a run that seemed to come out of the hillside. A small pool of cold water welled up at its base.

He stopped Colonel Ben nearby under a shade tree and dismounted. Alisha waited until he turned back to help her. When she stepped off the carriage, she wrapped her arms around his neck and said, "We are not being watched now."

They suspended the bottles of lemonade in the spring. They spread the blanket under another tree and sat down. "There will be people coming in after church. It is a popular place to have a Sunday picnic. It is private land. I think it belongs to someone in Maggie's family."

"Where in the world did you get the lemons? he asked.

"You forget Florida is in the Confederacy. Blockade runners get them through various ways. We use them to make lemon-flavored milk for the patients. We get sugarloaf the same way."

She still had the encounter with the Confederate Rangers on her mind. "You meant that!" she exclaimed. "If I had not been there, you would have shot it out with all six of those men. What makes you like that?" she asked, as if she had just realized the full meaning of his earlier statements regarding the morning's meeting with the Confederates.

"I simply meant I would protect myself, and you. A man never knows what he will do until he is presented with the problem. Yet, I always try to think ahead. Please, I do not want to lose your friendship or your trust. My job will take me away, but I will always come back. I will always come back until you tell me not to. But, you should know that I have something I must do."

"What is your cross that you bear?"

"I have vowed to hunt down the man responsible for the deaths of my aunt and uncle. That is my only cross to bear," he stated emphatically.

To change the subject he asked, "How long have we known each other?"

"Ten days. Four encounters, and thanks to Kathryn Tompkins, I have been hugging, and kissing on you each time."

"Aunt Eppie had an old saying that I heard her say many times: 'All is well that ends well,'" he grinned.

"That sounds like Eppie Smith?" Alisha asked. "She used to say that."

"I think Smith was her first husband's name. She married Uncle Granville, after Smith died in a run-away-horse accident."

"Yes she did. She was my teacher in the lower grades. She quit teaching to marry her childhood sweetheart. He was an explorer, a mountain man, and a Santa Fe Trader. He returned and bought a farm across the river from Massanutten Mountain. They got back together after all those years," Alisha said.

She continued, "My parents wrote me that Eppie and her husband had been murdered by renegades a few months ago. My parents thought that the grandson had escaped the murderers and left the area."

"I am Granville's grandnephew. I was like a grandson to them. I did escape, and I intended to go west, but other things keep happening to me. I will tell you the story of their death sometime, but not today. Today is a time for happier things. Things such as a picnic, and lemonade, flowers to pick, and maybe some more of that hugging and kissing you were talking about."

"Stephen Purcell, you can be so innocent and green one moment, and so worldly the next." She laughed as she said it.

Chapter 15

They were behind schedule. The line move and two stream crossings had added some extra time. Smith and Bean drove their wagon to the rail station junction with Purcell, and retrieved a shipment containing a new desk, a counter, and a divider railing, custom made to the measurements Purcell had wired. A spare reel of wire made up their load. He wired McCorkle from the railroad junction and informed him that the Warrenton station would be ready for the new operator by the end of the week.

It was almost dinner time. Since Mrs. Tompkin's inn was near, the crew decided to go to the inn to have their noon meal. Purcell warned Smith and Bean to be very careful as to what they said, and to discuss none of the previous confrontations with Rebel Rangers. He wished to present themselves as noncombatants. They carried arms to protect themselves and that was all. He emphasized that the delightful lady was a southern belle and that was the way it was.

Upon arrival, Kathryn Tompkins met them at the door. She promptly hugged Purcell. He introduced Smith and Bean to her. She had them wash up and seated the three of them.

"I hear that you and Alisha have been seen together about town. That is wonderful. I am hearing how beautiful she is, and what a nice couple you make."

"She is an amazing person. I am better for having met her. I have you to thank for that."

They enjoyed a meal of fried chicken, mashed potatoes, gravy, and new peas. A large slice of apple pie finished the meal. Bean and Smith vowed to come back again.

Soon Purcell and the crew were back on the road with the new equipment. They passed the pole-setting crew on the way in. There were still more poles to be replaced. Bean and Smith dropped off to help that crew, and Purcell drove the wagon on in with his horse tied to the rear of the wagon. Farley and Purcell unloaded the wagon and worked on the depot building with the railroad crew. It was to be a joint railroad and telegraph office. Purcell enjoyed working with carpenter tools. It reminded him of his time with Granville.

The next day just before noon, a railroad crewman called for Purcell to come out of the building to greet his visitor. To Purcell's surprise he found a smiling Alisha sitting on a horse in front of the building. She was holding a veiled straw hat and the now familiar basket. "Maggie loaned me her horse and sidesaddle to bring you something to eat. I have good news concerning the Jennings boy."

Purcell led the horse to a dismounting stone, and she stepped off. He helped her negotiate the steps on down. Alisha said, "Mr. Farley, I brought enough for you to eat with us, should you wish to?" Farley excused himself, saying he usually went to the hotel to eat dinner when he was in town. She asked Purcell, "Where did the railroad crew go?"

"They are over on the north side, in the shade of the building. The sun is getting hotter. Summer is here. They hunt shade when they eat their noon meal. We can have our own private dining room in here. I will open the opposing windows and we will get a nice breeze. We have a chair and bench. I will move the table over there and you can have the chair. I will take the bench."

Alisha said, "I will sit on the bench with you. But, first I have some news." She looked over her shoulder, then wrapped her arms around his neck. She whispered, "The letter has been delivered. His parents know Harvey is safe and in good hands. They are very relieved and happy." She gave him a long kiss. "You are their hero, and mine. I have more news from home, but it can wait until after we eat."

She spread a cloth on the bench side of the table. She deftly laid out fried chicken on a platter. Then came two plates. A third with three oven-baked potatoes completed the main meal. Butter, bread, and apple sauce finished the picnic. She took a seat on the bench and motioned for him to sit beside her. They chatted and bantered. Purcell could not remember when he enjoyed a noon meal as much.

When they were done eating she took hold of his arm gently. "My parent's letter had news of your aunt and uncle Coldiron. A few days after you met with Moses Washington in the cornfield, he decided that the bodies should be moved from the shallow graves and properly buried. Moses and Bos Hartley went to the mill owner in Port Republic, and asked his help. They figured since the Confederacy was obtaining flour and meal from him that he could be a helpful influence if they got into trouble for moving the graves.

"The mill owner was more than willing to help, since he knew both Granville and Eppie. He got a group of people together. They removed the bodies from the shallow graves. Eppie and Granville received a proper burial in the Port Republic cemetery. A local minister conducted graveside services. Many of their friends were there, including my grandparents."

Purcell sat silent for a long time. Finally he said, "I have worried about the graves. I am relieved and thankful. I still intend to find and kill the man responsible for their deaths."

"I had guessed as much. I will not discourage, or encourage that. I can just hope that your quest for revenge does not interfere with our relationship. All I can do is hope that you don't get hurt. We must wait until this frightful war is over, anyhow." Suddenly she had to find something for her hands to do. She started clearing the table and repacking the basket.

"If it interferes with us I will drop the quest," Purcell said. "Nothing is more important to me than you are. You have taken the place in my life occupied by my aunt and uncle, only in a very different way. I have known that almost from our first meeting. My life has changed." Suddenly he knew he could not stop there. "Will you marry me?" He could not believe he said that. But he did, and he meant it. Suddenly he was afraid it was too soon to propose marriage. "I apologize, perhaps it is too soon for me to ask? Maybe I should give you more time?"

She smiled to put him at ease. "Stephen Purcell, of course I will marry you. I have thought of nothing else but you for days! I should inform my parents of our intentions before we make our engagement known to others."

They stood and embraced again. Farley stepped into the open door and quickly stepped back out.

Alisha put on her hat with the sun shading veil and reluctantly made ready to leave. Purcell took her hand and the basket. They walked back out to the horse. He again led it to the block. "Thank you for the news and the dinner. Tomorrow is Saturday?"

"Six o'clock unless we have an emergency. Either of us," she added. She stopped the horse and turned it back toward Purcell. "Perhaps we should go to church Sunday. I am suddenly getting a lot of interest from several gentlemen. If we go to church, I think that will stop. Here, a woman does not take her beau to church with her unless it is serious. I just want to get them off my case."

"Suddenly they have seen what a pretty lady you are," he explained.

"I am your lady. They should look elsewhere. I wish to belong to no one else." She placed her hand in front of the veil to indicate a blown kiss, then turned the horse and left.

From inside the door, Farley said, "Man that was plain enough, even I could understand it. I hope I can find a woman like that."

"You will, Farley. Maybe when you least expect it. Just as it has happened for me." Purcell stood and watched her until she rode out of sight. "Farley, I have never met a girl like her. She is so strong-willed one moment, and the next moment so tender and loving."

"Don't you reckon it has something to do with being a nurse?" Farley replied.

"Maybe so. Right now, she is my nurse. How I could be so lucky, I do not know."

Purcell returned to the work at hand. He realized he was rushing things. His world was changing and he would adapt to it. For the love of a woman like that one, every man should. Suddenly he was beginning to question his resolve to find and kill Striker.

Did he really want to go west? He had listened many times to the old man's description of the vast, almost endless grasslands. The mountain landscapes of tall trees and rushing streams tumbling down into fertile valleys. Would he ever see it? Well, he did not intend to leave Alisha for the gentlemen to pester. That had happened to Granville and Eppie the first time around.

Purcell and Alisha took Saturday supper at the hotel, and spent the rest of the evening talking and wondering when the war would end and what they would do when it did. They could not make long-term plans. They decided that they both wished to return home to the Shenandoah Valley. They knew that would be impossible until the conflict was over. After that, they would marry and decide then what to do with the rest of their lives.

Purcell and Alisha went to the brush arbor church service. That did attract a lot of attention, and tongues were wagging as Alisha had predicted. For their Sunday evening they drove Colonel Ben down to Kathryn's inn, took supper, and visited until late. They drove back in the dark with only the moon for company.

The next morning, Purcell sent the crews back to Brandy Station. He instructed Smith to hook the wire in at the railroad junction on his way through. The new operator had not shown up. Purcell planned to stay and operate the equipment until the operator arrived. Purcell would instruct Farley on the operation of the telegraph, including the Morse Code. He wired McCorkle of his plans, as soon as he determined that the equipment was live. McCorkle wired back his consent.

Each day Purcell would go in and have his noon meal with Alisha in the basement kitchen of the hospital. She would send back a meal for Farley. Purcell would always leave money for the meals.

He was in the telegraph office part of the depot, when he picked up on a coded military communication. He remembered enough of the cipher to make out that General Hunter was moving on Staunton.

He did not know what to do. Alisha's family lived in Staunton. He wanted to tell Alisha, but it would be dangerous, as well as unethical, for him to disclose military information. By the time he saw her at noon the next day, he could tell she already knew. For the first time he saw tears on her cheeks.

"The Union army is looting and burning Staunton," she said.

"The information I am hearing is that they are to burn military supplies and manufacturing, not homes," he said, trying to reassure her.

"Who can ever be sure?" she asked. In the kitchen he held her close, oblivious to the cooks and workers coming and going. Finally, she told him to go, that she would be all right. He picked up Farley's meal and went back to the depot.

The noon train made its first run in and left the new railroad/telegraph agent. The train crew turned the train around, using the newly-repaired triangle turn around. Purcell hoped that this time opposing forces would not destroy the spur and turnaround. He had personal reasons to worry.

Purcell spent the afternoon getting the new agent oriented and settled in to the hotel. The agent would stay there until he found another place to his liking.

Purcell did not want to leave, but he must notify McCorkle that the new man had arrived. He sent the wire late and went back the next morning to get the reply. The wire came in from McCorkle instructing
Purcell and Farley to continue the line inspection. McCorkle had obtained railroad passes for them and their horses.

They were to take the first train available to Alexandria. Then they would work their way back to Warrenton and then on back to Brandy Station. They were to work six days, with Sundays off until they finished. McCorkle instructed them to report to the Alexandria Telegraph Office and pick up additional traveling funds.

He went by the church to tell Alisha he was leaving for

awhile. She greeted him with the news that General Hunter had left Staunton. He had gone to Lexington and burned the Virginia Military Institute.

"Do you have news of your family?" he inquired.

"No. Not a thing. I imagine any communication will be scarce for a time."

"I have just got a new assignment. We must put our horses on the train, go to Alexandria, and start back. We will be inspecting telegraph line, and making repair and construction notes. While I am in Alexandria, I am to meet with the main area supervisor. My assignment could change."

"Do you know how long?"

"I figure a week, perhaps two at the most."

Together they figured out how they would communicate. He would send letters. If he was sure of his route he would give her the locations of the telegraph offices. She could send letters for the office to hold for him. They would use telegrams if the letter arrangement did not work. A telegram would not be private. So they would use them sparingly.

"When do you leave?" Alisha asked.

"Tomorrow morning. We load the horses at the junction siding and ride with them to Alexandria. I think that is probably about fifty miles. We could be back by the weekend after next. I can come back by here. However, they probably won't let me headquarter here. I will figure something out."

"I want you near, if you can be. You should not worry if you are not. I will be here," Alisha assured him.

The next morning they went to the junction siding. After a short wait, the north bound train pulled off, and the train crew brought a stock car alongside the ramped loading dock. The car was equipped with padded stalls and sawdust covered floors. A crewman commented, "General Sheridan's horses have ridden in this car. His horse Rienzi always rides in this stall. Your horse is about the same size, maybe a little smaller. You can always say your horse rode in Rienzi's stall."

"I have observed the general's horse up close. My horse is at least a half a hand taller, if not more. He has a lot better conformation. Look at my horse's head, and then look at Rienzi's head next time you see him. Rienzi is narrow between the ears with a Roman nose. Not the most desirable head on a horse," Purcell retorted.

Colonel Ben stepped right in. Farley's black horse took a little persuading. Once in, the black settled down. They put him in the stall next to the Colonel.

"You can ride in the back car if you wish. There is seating there," the crewman gingerly offered. He decided not to tell them that was where the general rode. Purcell and Farley decided to stay with their mounts and gear. They were thinking it was best to keep their rifles close.

"I don't reckon he will slight your horse again," Farley laughed.

"I guess I came on a bit strong," Purcell admitted. "Striker and his men were after me, trying every day to kill me. They pursued me for weeks. I had no weapon and very little to eat. Colonel Ben was the only protection I had. He outran them and carried me out of harm's way. Between me and him, we outsmarted and outmaneuvered the murdering thieves every time they came close. We beat them at their own game. All that said, Rienzi is a good war horse. I am sure the general feels just as strongly about him as I do about Colonel Ben."

With some noise and smoke the train switched onto the main track. Purcell laid the wagon sheet out along the side where he could see through the slatted wall of the stock car. He sat on the canvas, leaned against the saddle, and watched the landscape slide by. Farley laid out on his bedroll and took a nap. After a stop at Manassas Junction, the train rolled on into the Alexandria switch yards.

Farley was familiar with the area and they soon had a place to stable the horses and lodge for the night. They reported to the telegraph office the next morning as instructed. The clerk asked Purcell to come into a private office.

The area supervisor's name was Brown. There was another important-looking individual with him. Purcell was surprised to learn that the visitor was Captain Thomas Eckert. He was Secretary of War Stanton's right-hand man. Eckert was the top boss of the American Telegraph Company, the military part of the telegraph. "I wanted to meet you Mr. Purcell. The wisdom of your telegrams conceal your young age. I have read some of your suggestions to your supervisor. I agree that the telegraph lines should parallel the railroads, for better utilization of both.

"General Grant personally holds you in high esteem. I also read a glowing report on how you outfoxed a group of Rebel ambushers on the Culpeper Pike, saving your crew from harm. You kept some valuable equipment from falling into enemy hands."

He continued, "Several years ago, I took passage on a ship to England. The captain's name was Purcell. I was sorry to hear later that his ship went down in a storm, with the loss of all hands. Could he be any relation?"

"Yes sir. He was my father," Purcell answered.

"I suspected as much. I became well acquainted with him. In fact, I dined at his table frequently on the voyage. I am sorry for your loss. He was looking forward to the day his son would follow in his footsteps and captain a ship."

"Yes, I know, but I guess it was not to be. I really do not think I want to, now."

"Well young man, you keep thinking about how we can put the telegraph to better use." Eckert shook hands with Purcell and excused himself. After Eckert left, the area supervisor noted that the Washington office monitored all telegraphs going in and out of that part of Virginia. Purcell did not bother to tell him that he already knew that.

Brown went to a safe and pulled out an envelope. He removed money and two pieces of paper. "Count the money, and sign one of the receipt slips. Keep the extra copy for your records. This is expense money. You are to return any monies left to your home area supervisor when you reach your home destination. Incidentally, they wanted me to tell you that your supervisor is holding last month's pay for you and Mr. Farley. You can pick that up when you get back in."

Chapter 16

Purcell and Farley left Alexandria, following the telegraph lines through Fairfax and on to Aldie. It took them three days to inspect and make notes on that section of line. At Aldie they were instructed by telegram to proceed on to Leesburg, then to Ball's Bluff on the upper Potomac, and eventually to Martinsburg. They also received word that Union General Hunter had been defeated at Lynchburg. His forces were retreating into the Allegheny Mountains of West Virginia. The Confederate Army, once again, had control of the Shenandoah Valley.

A few days later, much to Purcell's dismay, the reports were that the vengeful Hunter was burning everything in his path as he retreated. He was not just burning manufacturing facilities and war support crops, he was also burning homes. Hunter now had the nickname "Black Dave." The home Purcell shared with Granville and Eppie had been destroyed. He could feel for the people. They could not defend themselves against either army. He worried for Alisha's family.

When they reached Martinsburg, they were instructed to return to Leesburg. Evacuation trains were being sent in on the Loudon and Hampshire Railroad. They were to load themselves and their horses on the first available train to Alexandria. The report was that the Confederate Armies of General Early and General Breckenridge were marching up the Shenandoah Valley, headed for Washington.

Farley and Purcell reported in at the telegraph office near the railroad yards in Alexandria. They were instructed to stable their horses, and stand by to repair and replace telegraph lines and equipment as needed. General Early was expected to attack Washington within the next few days.

The telegraph supervisor obtained lodging for Purcell and Farley, and continued to let them work as a team. They were put up at Gadsby's Tavern on Royal Street. The supervisor advised that they should avoid the Marshall House and Tavern. When asked why, he related the story of the overzealous New York Fire Zouave officer who had removed a secessionist flag from the hotel's roof-mounted flagpole. The tavern owner had promptly shot him on the staircase. The Zouaves then killed the owner on the spot. Four years later, bad feelings still existed about the incident.

As a youngster living in New York, Purcell had watched the Fire Zouaves march in patriotic parades. Their uniforms were colorful, if not a bit outlandish. Most of the military units were made up of volunteer New York firemen. He could well believe that some of them would make a move on the Rebel flag.

Alexandria was a key rail center and shipping harbor. It was a secessionist town, but it was of strategic importance to the Union. It had remained occupied by Union troops since the War of the Rebellion had started.

Purcell and Farley set about checking line between the various forts surrounding Washington. They were still charged with finding wire taps and apprehending "telegraph spies," as the supervisor liked to call them.

Purcell wrote Alisha, giving her his new address. They agreed to write each other once a week. Purcell was careful not to give her too much information about what he was doing. Their letters mostly talked about how much they missed each other, and how much they hoped that the war would soon be over. She longed to return to the Shenandoah. Purcell wanted to return her there as soon as possible.

Farley's family was in Pennsylvania, so he had no problem getting letters out to them. McCorkle was trying very hard to get his employees back into their home area. Purcell figured that McCorkle was worrying about Farley. Purcell wired McCorkle that they were doing okay. He noted that his teammate was proving to be very reliable. He assured McCorkle that he wanted to get back to his home area as soon as possible. He did not discuss the fact in the telegram, but he knew that headquarters would not release them until after the crisis in Washington was over. He surmised that McCorkle also knew that.

Because several of the the bridges had been burned, Purcell and Farley worked south of the Potomac River. Ferry boats operated as temporary crossings, if needed. The area supervisor provided a Remington revolver for Farley to carry. Purcell located some extra ammunition for his Henry and Farley's Spencer. Purcell was hoping that they would not need it. If General Early decided to move east, every man that could stand would be pressed into service.

As Early's Confederates drew closer, the telegraph crews were forced to cut wire and drop the Confederate occupied areas. Purcell learned that the

Confederate forces had taken Martinsburg. The Confederates replenished their dwindling supplies from Federal warehouses and then burned the warehouses.

Purcell and Farley were busy repairing and stringing telegraph lines for the command posts. They kept their weapons and the horses no more than a few steps away. The horses' saddles were not removed at night and each man kept his horse's picket rope tied around his wrist. In the turmoil the horses could be lost or stolen. Purcell was not about to let that happen.

Confederate troops attacked Ft. Stevens on the northwestern outskirts of Washington. At Ft. Stevens, Confederate General Early was in sight of the Capitol building. Purcell and Farley were so busy working on communication lines that they had little time to think about the dangerous place they were in.

After two days of bitter fighting, Union General Lew Wallace's troops repelled the Confederates. With Union reinforcements pouring into Washington, General Early gave up his quest to capture the capital. By July 14, the battle for Washington was over. Early quietly faded away into the Shenandoah Valley to fight again, later. He accomplished one of his goals, which was to divert some of General Grant's troops from southern Virginia, and relieve some pressure on General Lee.

The back-and-forth skirmishes and battles left the railroads and telegraph lines in shambles. Purcell and Farley worked with other crews getting the telegraph back in operation. Purcell found himself running crews. Usually the men were older and more experienced, but no one questioned his authority. More than once he heard the phrase "Shenandoah Sharpshooter" whispered behind his back.

After several weeks of work, the telegraph lines were back in operation. General Lew Wallace commended Purcell and his repair crews for fast and efficient work. As soon as the downed lines went up Purcell and Farley went back to patrolling and inspecting the restored line.

The summer was hot and uncomfortable, and the fall months were not proving much better. Purcell and Farley were returning to Alexandria from a patrol of several days length, when Purcell spotted a new line constructed down a side street. "Farley, was that line there when when we left last Monday?"

"No, I don't think so. There is nothing down that street but a few storefronts and some small tenant houses."

"The lines and poles are from our storage yard. See the inventory chalk marks? No anchors. Not even a slack span. It is temporary at the best. Let us go have a look."

They followed the line a few hundred yards to a store front advertising a seamstress. The sign on the door said closed.

"Hold the horses, I am going to check the rear," Purcell said to Farley. "Give me a minute to get around behind. Then make a lot of noise. We will see what happens." Purcell moved around behind the building and approached the door.

At the front of the building, Farley raised a racket, swearing at his "knot headed" horse.

Purcell tried the door and it opened into a back room. A younger man was at a telegraph key, and another man dressed in a rough homespun suit sat at a desk. The man at the desk had his back to Purcell. It was obvious that they had not heard Farley because of the closed front room. The man in the suit turned slowly to face Purcell and the muzzle of the Henry.

Purcell recognized the Rebel ranger, Captain McNeill, from the roadside incident on the way to Alisha's picnic. Purcell was sure that both individuals would be armed, although no weapons were in sight. McNeill said, "Well Shenandoah, we meet again."

Purcell said, "Tell your man that I have seen that look in a man's eyes before. He should not go for his gun."

"You heard the man Lane, stand down."

"Send him out to tighten your cinches," Purcell instructed.

McNeill nodded to the man he called Lane. Lane got up and left quietly.

"Captain, I am going to return a favor," Purcell said. "However, I must destroy your handy little setup here. Now get up and leave quickly."

McNeill complied, stopping at the door. "I delivered a wounded man to the hospital a few days ago. While there, I saw a lonely, but otherwise happy young woman. She is in good health. You are a very lucky man." He went through the door. As it was on the road that day, he was gone.

Purcell returned to the street and an anxious Farley. "There were two of them. They went out after I went in. I did not want to shoot when I saw no guns. I won't back shoot a man. There is a sending and receiving unit in there. Hand me your pliers, and I will take it loose and we will carry it with us. A construction crew can remove the line tomorrow."

The horsemen rode quickly and quietly down the alley. After they had put a safe distance between them and the man with the repeating rifle, Lane broke the silence. "What just happened back there, Captain?"

"Once, I let a man live, because I liked him. He just returned the courtesy."

"That has probably happened many times in this old war," Lane said.

"I reckon it has. In such instances, it is best for a man to keep his own counsel." They rode on in silence.

Purcell and Farley reported to Brown, describing the tap that they had found. Brown expressed disbelief. "How could they have got into the yard without the night watchman seeing them?"

Purcell offered an explanation. "They probably removed the poles and wire during the daylight. Who would question a crew's right to be there in the light of day? The yardmen may have even helped load the materials. They would have to show a work material's ticket, but that would be easy to make. They would have built the line in daylight. The bogus crew probably waved at the regulars as they went by."

"That took guts and planning. They would have pulled it off, if not for you guys. You are worth having around, but they aren't going to let me keep you," Brown lamented. "Farley, you are to go back to your crew chief at Brandy Station. Purcell, you will report to the Secretary of War Office in Washington. The rumor is you are going to head a special projects crew."

"When are we to report?" Purcell asked.

"They are going to give you both a week off. You will need to take your horses back to Brandy Station. Purcell, you can go into Washington anytime. Farley, if you want to go visit your family, Purcell can take your horse back with him."

There was not a railroad bridge across the Potomac into Washington. Farley rode with Purcell in a taxi service hack across the Long Bridge to the Washington rail terminal, and then rode the train to Baltimore and on into Pennsylvania. Purcell got off the carriage at Staunton's office and met again with the Telegraph Supervisor Eckert.

Eckert told him that the service was planning a test application of a new waterproof wire covering called gutta percha. They wished to install a crossing on the Potomac River at the small seaport of Belle Plain. A second crossing would be made a short distance up Aquia Creek. They wanted him to oversee the project. Purcell would be furnished a steam-powered tugboat and an experienced crew. He could take a few days off before the project started. When the project started it would go non-stop. The wire was to be laid on the bottom of the creek and the Belle Plain Harbor before bad weather set in.

The covered wire was to be attached to regular telegraph batteries, charged with voltage, and tested frequently throughout the winter. If the line withstood the the rugged winter it would be laid at all river crossings. Purcell was surprised to learn that his wages had been raised to $60 per month. He could continue to work out of Brandy Station and the Warrenton area. He did not let his emotions show, but he was happy. The project would keep him in the area. He could could see Alisha more often.

Purcell took a hack back across to Alexandria and prepared to board a train with the horses. He would disembark at the spur to Warrenton. He checked into the Warren Green Hotel late and took a sandwich at the bar for supper. He took a bath in the bathhouse and retired. He was tired but happy. Tomorrow he would see Alisha.

The next morning he gave a youngster hanging around the livery two bits to deliver a note to Alisha. He rode over to the railroad telegraph office and checked in there. While there, he sent a telegram to McCorkle telling him he would be returning on Monday.

Purcell spent the day at the telegraph office. The youngster who delivered Purcell's note that morning brought an answer from Alisha. The note suggested that they spend the weekend at Kathryn Tompkin's inn. If he agreed, he was to pick her up at the hospital at around five-thirty.

That evening, Purcell left the depot, went to the livery, and arranged for the rental buggy.

Promptly, he arrived behind the church at the appointed time and went in the rear door. Alisha was waiting, very calm and collected.

"Would you please help me with my overnight luggage," she asked. He went in to get it, and heard the door close behind him. "You will never know how much I have missed you," she said.

"Oh yes, I do," he replied.

"Well then, we had better start doing some of that hugging and kissing, you like so much! Kathryn won't give us much privacy, once we are there."

They arrived at the Inn, and Kathryn showed them to their rooms. She set up the side dining room for them so they could dine and talk privately. Kathryn had noticed how well Colonel Ben handled the buggy. "That old livery buggy is terribly worn and plain. You need a better buggy for that fancy horse."

"That must wait," Purcell reminded her.

"Do you know what you are going to do when this horrible war is over?"

"No, my uncle told me the day he died, that the farm had been transferred to me. I will go back there and check that out. From then on we will make our plans accordingly."

Before Kathryn could ask, Alisha said, "We do plan to marry. We thought we would tell you first.

My mother has already read between the lines, and has informed me that I am going to have a church wedding at home. I wrote back and said that was what we both wanted. We will make those decisions when the time comes."

They spent the weekend visiting with Kathryn, strolling around the gardens and orchards. The farmhands were harvesting corn and pumpkins. The turnips had green tops, and would be harvested as the weather grew cooler. Purcell was certain that it was good for Alisha to get away from the hospital.

On the way back into Warrenton, he stopped at the railroad depot and picked up a Washington paper. General Sheridan's troops were burning crops, mills, barns, and other Rebel support facilities between Staunton and Harrisburg.

The complete devastation of the widest part of the valley had been accomplished. It was an area of approximately forty miles long and twenty-five miles wide. The news brought tears to Alisha's eyes. She could only hope her family had escaped the carnage.

At Brandy Station, McCorkle was glad to see Purcell. He had brought Purcell's bunk from the granary to the cabin for the winter. McCorkle planned to spend part of his time working out of his Pennsylvania home. Purcell inquired about Harvey Jennings, and found that McCorkle had put him to work in the telegraph office after Williams had quit and went back north. Jennings was living with Adams and his family. "He is a talkative little feller, but he works as fast as he talks. He is trustworthy. No one has questioned his southern origin. I have had good luck with those Shenandoah Valley youngsters," McCorkle laughed.

Purcell's back pay came in Greenbacks. He would have rather had it in Double Eagles. The telegraph was generous with the travel expenses, and he was able to save most of his salary. The next time he visited Alexandria, he planned to purchase a good suit of clothes. He hid most of his money at the bottom of the locked toolbox.

Purcell relocated to Belle Plain to start Eckert's project. He found a room and meals with a local family. Their names were Joe and Polly Hall. They had two children. They were a little reserved at first, but warmed up to him when they realized he was from the Shenandoah Valley. His nickname had followed him to Belle Plain.

The engineers had the wire and materials shipped in from New York by boat. The materials and equipment were stored in a warehouse near Belle Plain. The wire length was continuous on the extra-large reels to eliminate the problem of making a watertight splice. The size of the reels and the mounting equipment would be almost more than the little boat could handle.

After examining the new experimental covering, Purcell thought he perceived a problem. The coating was lighter than the familiar rubber coated type. Although the lighter covering would help with the tug's weight problem, it would be more buoyant in the water. He immediately telegraphed Eckert's office, with his assessment of the problem. He indicated that he thought that the cable would be influenced by the stream current as well as the rise and fall of the tide. In short, the wire needed weight.

A telegraph came back asking for his recommendation. Purcell's first thought was, where was an engineer when he needed him? He sat, and stared at the wall for awhile, weighing the problem. He wired Eckert's office asking for a thousand pounds of lead sheet, approximately one-forth inch thick. At the points where the stream's current would be greatest, the crew could install two inch wide strips of lead placed around the wire at intervals, in corkscrew fashion. He concluded the telegram with the explanation that the soft lead would not harm the covering. The effect would be similar to the weighting of a fisherman's net.

A telegram came back, indicating the lead would be sent as soon as it could be located. The crew set about placing the four small equipment buildings, one at the end of each crossing site. Termination poles would also be set while they were waiting on the lead.

The wire would be buried from the water to the pole at one site, and laid on the ground at the other site. Wire was ran out to the pole.

The batteries and test equipment were set up, ready to go. They had the installation ready to lay wire by late Friday afternoon. Purcell released the crew until Monday morning.

Purcell visited around the town Saturday afternoon. He went out of his way to explain that he was testing materials, and that the application was not a working telegraph. He was sure that Partisan Rangers were in the area, and he surmised that the equipment would be safer if they knew it was not a working telegraph. Purcell even went to church on Sunday.

The following Monday the lead sheeting arrived on a boat by mid morning. It took the rest of the day to get a reel mounted on the tug and ready to lay out wire. They cut strips of lead from some of the sheeting, and got it ready to install. Purcell had a good crew, two boisterous Irishmen, two equally likable Germans, and the tugboat captain.

One of the Germans came up with the idea of forming the lead weights by twisting them into the corkscrew configuration around a mandrel rod. Once they got the hang of it, the job progressed nicely. They finished the entire project by the end of the week. They were a week ahead of Eckert's timetable. Purcell said goodbye to the Hall family and went back to Brandy Station.

Chapter 17

The winter passed slowly. McCorkle was gone every other week. During his absence, he was in Pennsylvania or Washington, and left the running of the Brandy Station area to Purcell and Murphy. Murphy worked in the Fredericksburg and Belle Plain area. He took care of the warehousing and supplying of materials to the southeastern battlefront. Purcell's crews supplied and backed up the military telegraphers for the Blue Ridge and Shenandoah area. Purcell ran tests on the underwater line near Belle Plain every two weeks. He would ride over there horseback, and return to Brandy Station the next day.

On the weekends that McCorkle was in, Purcell would go over to Warrenton to attend church with Alisha. Afterward they would sit and talk for hours. She had heard from the upper valley.

Her parents and their home at Staunton was safe. The grandparents at Port Republic were also safe. The Federal Cavalry under General Custer had burned the mills and crops at Port Republic. Several homes caught fire, but Custer's troops actually helped the people fight the home fires. The burning of the mills, along with the previous destruction of the bridge crossing the Shenandoah by Confederate General Jackson, had left the community in a hopeless condition.

Alisha had other war news. Captain McNeil had been killed in a battle at Mt. Jackson. Gilmore had been captured. Mosby was still operating, striking federal supply lines. She noted that she had heard no news of Alvin Striker.

"He seems to have disappeared." She watched for Purcell's reaction as she said it.

He shrugged his shoulders, "Striker is around, like the snake he is. He has probably crawled into a hole for the winter. Early has moved out of the valley, and the Union is in control of the entire Shenandoah. Perhaps I will eventually learn something of Striker's location."

Back at McCorkle's cabin, Purcell sat and stared into the fire. He thought about Striker, and mulled over his own vow of revenge. Purcell was not one to give up easily. But he knew Alisha did not want him to pursue Striker. Well, he decided he would just put it away and not think about it any more.

The earth was beginning to warm up. It was time to start Eppie's plants. He wished he was there at the farmstead. He would go back. Alisha's father was a lawyer. She had told him that her father would help him run the paperwork down. Granville had said there was paperwork. Would it be at the courthouse? Some courthouses and records had been burned. And then there was the land Granville owned in the New Mexico territory.

Purcell wondered if he should work the farm? There were no tools to speak of. After the raiders had failed at carrying off the anvil in their first raid, Purcell and Granville had worked some skids under the anvil, hooked Colonel Ben to it, dragged it into the timber, and hid it. Tillage and iron hand tools are what Purcell needed. There would be some blacksmith tongs and hand tools that survived the fire. He could put a forge together and make some tools. The double-shovel cultivator would probably be laying where they dropped it in the potato patch.

One of the field wagons had survived the first raid and fire. Again Granville had used Ben and their own muscle to drag it to a rock overhang on the mountainside to hide and protect it from the weather. It too, was probably still there. A walking plow was in the spring cave where the livestock had been hidden. He would need more equipment than that.

The McCormick reaper that Granville was so proud of was nothing but a pile of rusted iron in the ashes of a burned shed. He could build a log home with his own hands and the horsepower he had. Without oxen, mules, or draft horses, he could not run much of a farm. Purcell began to think the situation was hopeless. He did not have the funds needed. Did he even want to try?

McCorkle sent Purcell and Bean to inspect and determine the material and crews needed to re-build the telegraph lines around Strasburg, and south to Mt. Jackson. The many back and forth skirmishes had torn the lines up badly.

While at Mt. Jackson, word reached them that Lee had surrendered to Grant. The war was all but over. They finished the inspection, took a shortcut through the Blue Ridge by Luray to Culpeper, and on into Brandy Station. It was nearly the same route Purcell took the year before. Along the way, it suddenly came to Purcell that he had forgotten his birthday again. He was now twenty-one years old.

When he reached Brandy station, there was a telegram from Alisha. She said to come and visit her as soon as he could. She explained that she had some family information to share with him. He knew that family was her way of letting him know she had information important to themselves. She was his family.

Purcell had to wait until the weekend to wrap things up. McCorkle let him leave Saturday morning. Purcell used his telegraph pass to put himself and his horse on the early northbound train. It pulled into the Warrenton spur siding and let him off. He unloaded his horse and made the short ride into Warrenton.

Purcell went directly to the church. He rode around to the rear and secured Ben in the shed barn with the hospital workers' horses. He entered the church through the basement kitchen door. He found Alisha and her supervising nurse Maggie sitting at a table drinking coffee.

Alisha arose and embraced him. Maggie politely looked the other way. They both invited him to sit down and have coffee.

Purcell said, "It is unusual to see the two of you leisurely drinking coffee."

"Business has slowed around here since the shooting stopped," Maggie replied.

"That is one of the things I wanted to tell you," Alisha said. "They have decided to close our hospital down. The congregation wants their building back. We will close and move out at the end of the month... So now we have to decide how we are going to proceed."

Maggie suggested, "Why don't you take him to your room where you can talk in private? The kitchen workers will be back in here soon."

"She is worrying about us. Any other time she would have scolded me for seeing you in my room."

In the privacy of the room they embraced again. "I am glad the war is over. However, I want to stay near you," she said.

"You can go home and I can follow in a few weeks." Purcell did not want her to leave, but he knew it was time she returned to her family.

"I thought that I might get work in the hospital at Alexandria, but those doctors there look down on female nurses. They segregated us here after the worst of the battles were over. You have noticed of course, we are now a convalescent hospital. The male nurses and worst causalities are over at the regular hospital."

She continued, "I think I may be able to work again with Doctor Walker at Harrisonburg. His experience with Florence Nightingale early in the Crimean War gave him a new perspective on women nurses. Poor man, he returned home to find his own country getting ready for a civil war."

Purcell said, "If you want to work in your chosen field, I want that also. However, you may want to take some time off to visit and relax with your parents. Don't worry about me, I will follow, until you tell me not to."

"I will never tell you not to. You know that," she smiled.

"Something else I want to tell you. I have given up hunting Striker. You, and that piece of land in our beautiful Shenandoah Valley are more important to me."

"Oh my goodness, that is the other reason for my telegram! Come with me, I have someone I want you to meet."

She explained further as they made their way between the beds. "He was wounded in the arm at the battle of Mt. Jackson. Gangrene set in and he finally came out of hiding. The doctors had to amputate the arm. He ended up over here. He was at Mt. Jackson with McNeil. Prior to joining McNeil, he rode with Striker for a short time. I didn't tell him anything about you. I just listened when he talked."

James Gooden was sitting in a chair looking at the changing landscape of spring through an open window. He was thinking of his home in Georgia.

How he wished he was there. His thoughts of home were interrupted when he heard the voice of that pretty nurse everybody fell in love with.

"Mr. Gooden, Mr. Gooden, are you awake? We have been giving him laudanum for pain. He may be a bit groggy."

The man turned in the chair carefully, holding on to the stub of what was left of his right arm.

"James Gooden, this is Stephen Purcell, my husband-to-be. Mr. Gooden is from Georgia."

"Suh, forgive me for not shak'n hands, I am still try'n to adjust to the lack of an arm." The man's thought process was a little muddled, but he remembered the name. "I think Suh, I have heard Captain McNeil speak of you. You are the one called the Shenandoah Sharpshooter? He said to run like hell, if we was to come up against you. And I agreed with him."

Purcell smiled. "Yes, it seems that nicknames and reputations have a way of sticking with us."

"Yes Suh. Sometimes they are good. Sometimes they are bad."

After a long pause, he said, "Shenandoah, we have met before, on the pike to Culpeper. You were the telegraph man with the long barreled repeater rifle. Were you not?"

Purcell nodded that he was. "I was in charge, that day."

"I heard you order them to cease fire, and to not back shoot us. I reckon I owe you my life." There was a long silence in the room. Then Gooden continued. "You sure did outsmart us that day. Striker did not expect you teamsters to stand and fight.

"We had two more men with horses back in the brush where we had been camped. All but one of the riderless horses came to the camp horses, so we loaded up the dead and got out of there. Striker was dead so we buried the four of them at Sperryville and joined up with McNeil."

Purcell was stunned by the information. "Striker is dead? Can you describe him for me?"

"I figured Striker was known to you? He was the lookout at the top of the hill the day we attacked your wagons. He had a long knife scar along his left jaw. Somebody tried for his throat, but missed. He was a knife fighter. He carried a bone handled knife with three notches in the handle. Claimed he had killed that many men with it. He was the man, til he crossed paths with you. A couple of the older Rangers were glad you killed him."

Purcell inhaled sharply, realizing he was carrying Striker's bone-handled knife on his belt. "One of my teamsters shot the man you describe," he explained. "Striker and some of his men killed my aunt and uncle on their farm across the river from Cross

Keys. I was a great distance up the hill when that occurred. I did not get a good look at him. Were you with him then?"

"No, I came here-a-bouts the week before we hit your wagons. If I was in on the kill'n, I would admit it. I understand that he chased you all over the mountains. He thought you was carrying money in a sack you had."

"Mr. Gooden, I am glad we did not shoot at you. And I am sorry for the loss of your arm. I am sure you will feel better when you get back home."

"I don't think so, I got word that Sherman burned our house."

Purcell was momentarily at a loss for words. Finally he said, "I am sorry. In my estimation Sherman has a lot in common with Striker." Purcell did not feel that the burning of homes, stealing, and pillaging was an admirable trait in any man. The color of his uniform did not excuse Striker or Sherman. Purcell's home had been burned, but he could rebuild it. This poor man would not be able to.

Purcell and Alisha visited awhile longer and excused themselves. They both knew the man was in pain, in more ways than one.

When they returned to the room, Alisha asked, "What do you think?"

"Striker would have killed me for my horse and a peck of potatoes. Anyway, I think a great weight has been lifted from my shoulders," he replied.

"I think it was lifted from your soul."

He knew that she was right.

They rented a buggy, and drove Colonel Ben out to Kathryn Tompkin's inn for supper. Purcell knew that the Virginia Central Railroad would soon be repaired and connected back up with the Orange and Alexandria Railroad. Alisha and Harvey Jennings could soon have a ride direct to Staunton, and then home.

Kathryn listened as they talked. They decided that Purcell would return to see Alisha off. He would give his notice and leave with the horses the following week after she left. He didn't say so, but he wanted to give her some time alone with her family before he showed up.

She leaned on his shoulder as they drove back. After awhile, she broke the silence. "Kathryn is giving us a carriage for a wedding gift. It has been stored in the barn since her husband left to fight for the Confederacy. She never took it out. I think it is the one they courted in. She asked if you had a team. It requires two horses."

"That is nice of her. The roan and gray are matched in size and disposition. They should make a good carriage team."

"I will telegraph you before you come back. If the carriage is ready you can bring the horses when you come. She is having her stable hand get it out and clean it up. I could wait and ride back home with you."

"It will be a two, maybe three day trip on the pike. On the railroad it will take less than half the time. You need a few days alone with your family."

She agreed, and commented that she would shop in Warrenton. She was considering taking the train to Alexandria to shop. "I want to put some clothes together before I leave. There is not much in the way of dry goods material left in Staunton. My mother is working on a wedding dress from material she has stored away."

They stood on the steps in an embrace for a long time. Finally she said, "I must go in."

Purcell returned the horse and buggy to the livery stable, and retired for the night at the hotel. He lay awake thinking for a long time. It was more difficult for him to leave her each time. Alisha was beautiful beyond words, but she was more to him than just a stunning woman. She was the most remarkable person he had ever met. She meant more to him than anyone. She made it plain that she felt the same way about him. He told her that he did not have much to offer her. Whatever happened, as she had said, it would happen to them, together.

When Purcell reached Brandy Station the next day, he had a telegram from the Pinkerton Agency wanting him to meet with their representative. It turned out to be a job offer. They thought he had demonstrated the skills needed to make a good detective. He thanked the man for the offer, but turned it down. Had he not met Alisha, he knew he would have accepted the job.

He did not have much to offer Alisha, but Granville and Eppie's life story had taught him a lesson. Eppie's family did not think Granville had much to offer, and Granville agreed. He went off to the frontier to make his fortune as a trapper and trader. Several years later, he made it back home to find Eppie had married another. She had waited for him, but she received word that he had died along a part of the Santa Fe Trail called the Jornada. Part of Granville's broken rifle and the mutilated body of his companion were found by a military patrol. They were sure that Granville had also met death at the hands of hostile Indians. She eventually married a local school teacher. Granville escaped from his Indian captors and finally returned home, too late. Heartbroken, he went back to work in the West.

Mose Washington was the one that brought word to Granville that Eppie's husband had been killed in a runaway horse accident. Granville dug up his cache of gold and silver coins and returned to the Shenandoah Valley. He bought his land and constructed a large log house. He imported some large Spanish Jacks and started raising mules.

After a proper interval Granville and Eppie married. Purcell did not intend for something like that to happen to himself and Alisha.

He submitted his resignation to McCorkle effective at the end of the month or soon thereafter. The American Telegraph Company sent a wire reminding him that there was much restoration work to be done in the southern part of the Shenandoah Valley. They were also contemplating considerable construction work to occur out West. They wanted him to check in with them when he had his personal affairs in order.

Two weeks later, he brought his team of horses to Kathryn's inn and picked up the carriage. Early the next morning, he loaded Alisha's belongings into the carriage and they drove to Brandy Station. Harvey Jennings and Alisha boarded the evening train. The train was due to arrive in Staunton the next afternoon.

Purcell worked in the telegraph office, replacing Harvey at the key. He knew that it would take them a few days to locate a permanent replacement.

On its return run, he met the train that Alisha and Harvey had taken home. The conductor confirmed they had arrived safely in Staunton. Purcell made his final plans to join them.

That evening, McCorkle called him out to the buggy shed. "You are going to need some tools on that farm, so Liz and I are going to make you a wedding present of this box of tools. Take the box loose from the wall, and we will load it in your carriage. Knowing you, I would bet you could build a house with those tools.

"It will take you three days to reach Staunton. Have you thought about the danger of traveling alone with three horses? People are desperate for horses right now."

Purcell explained, "I figure on camping and staying with the horses. I don't guess I will get a lot of sleep."

"Well, the crew and I have talked about it. You need somebody to watch your back. We have need to do some more line inspection on up the valley. Your traveling buddy Farley has volunteered to go along with you. When you get there, he will get on the train at Staunton and come back. No argument now. It is a done deal."

"I will not argue, McCorkle. Your wife told me when we first met, that behind the gruff exterior and all that red hair and beard, lurked the kindest Scotsman I would ever meet. She was right."

"Don't go getting all teary-eyed on me," McCorkle chuckled. "You better hunt Farley up and tell him when you plan to leave."

They decided that one would ride Colonel Ben and the other would drive the team. This would give them more flexibility if they were set upon. For some, the war was not over. It wouldn't be for several years. Each carried a side arm and a repeating rifle. They would alternate positions.

They departed early in the morning, taking the road west out of Brandy Station. They crossed Ruppins Run and forded the Hazel River. Not wanting to be in the mountains in the dark, Purcell stopped early. They pulled the carriage several yards off the road and made camp just out of Sperryville.

Purcell had followed Murphy's lead and outfitted himself with some camp utensils. They nailed the feed boxes to a large fallen log and grained the horses. Farley took the first watch and woke Purcell at midnight to take the rest of the night guard.

At sunrise, Purcell set about frying some bacon and eggs for breakfast. Purcell smiled to himself as he broke the eggs into the skillet. They had used another Murphy trick and packed the eggs in sawdust to keep them from breaking. He hoped he would get to see the tough Irishman again, sometime.

Farley woke to the smell of breakfast. He arose, and grained the horses again. After breakfast, they pulled up the grain boxes, and gave the horses more time to graze some grass. Two riders passed by quietly and did not look in their direction. It was obvious that the horsemen did not want to be seen. Purcell and Farley decided to move on quickly. They did not intend to give the strangers time to set up an ambush.

They traveled on into Sperryville and found the two riders stopped along the road at the outskirts of the town. Farley stopped the team and picked up his rifle. Purcell pulled his from the saddle boot.

Both men raised their hands to show they were empty. The near one said, "We wondered who you were, but when I saw you on that big horse, I realized you were the guy they call The Shenandoah Sharpshooter. We were orderlies at the Hill House. It has been about a year ago. We are kind of dreading to ride through the mountains by ourselves. Could we travel with you?"

"You look familiar," Purcell said. "Who was the officer the doctor sent you after?"

"Major George Forsyth. You looked bad, with blood all over you. It appears your wounds have healed."

"Are you armed?"

"No, that is why we wanted to ride along with you."

"Ride on ahead, and let my partner and I talk it over."

After they moved out, Purcell asked Farley for his input. Farley indicated it would be all right with him, if Purcell knew them.

Purcell thought for a moment. He had stayed at the Hill Mansion for about two weeks. After he got a good look at them, he did remember the men. They were medical orderlies, and he had taken meals at the cook house with them several times. Purcell figured that there was some safety in larger numbers. He signaled them to wait.

The riders introduced themselves. Their names were William Bates and Christopher Rust. They were being transferred to the Federal unit stationed at New Market.

Purcell figured that the twenty miles through Thornton Gap and the Blue Ridge would take most, if not all, of the day. They camped for the night near Luray. The medics shared night watch, and contributed beef jerky and coffee to the breakfast. Bates and Rust stopped at New Market. Purcell and Farley purchased an early lunch at a roadhouse and restocked their supplies. The carriage, and poor condition of the road, had slowed them down. Purcell had two more days before he would see Alisha and meet her family.

Anna Stewart worried about her daughter's upcoming marriage. These were difficult times. Her daughter's husband-to-be was leaving employment to come back to the valley. She decided to discuss her concerns with Alisha.

"Mother, he is like no man I have ever met. I will go with him wherever he goes. I have complete confidence in him."

"He has the reputation of being a gunman," her mother noted. "The Jennings boy said he shot that criminal right between the eyes. Not that he did not deserve it. I admit."

"He saved Harvey's life. He is a bigger-than-life hero to Harvey. Harvey is a bit over dramatic."

"There was a newspaper article from Alexandria, about a shootout in Warrenton Junction. Well, I worry. You followed one man to Warrenton, you know. Now you say you will follow this one anywhere."

"Mother, I followed that man because I was not sure of him. I will follow this one anywhere he wants me to, because I am sure of him."

"Okay, I won't say any more... How old is he?"

"He is three months older than I am."

"With all that experience, I thought he would be older."

"He is older. War matures people. Stephen and I have both seen things, and had to do things, that would never happen in other times."

"I know. I worried about you constantly. It was all I could do to keep Bea from going to Warrenton, too. As soon as the Female Academy opens back up she plans to attend. Well, strip down to your petticoats, and we will try this dress on again... You bought those nice underthings at Alexandria?"

Purcell and Farley arrived in Staunton late in the afternoon of the fourth day. At the railroad station, they checked the train schedules and found that Farley must layover a day. They went across the street and took rooms at the American Hotel. The clerk told them that members of the Stewart and Jennings family had been inquiring if they were in. Purcell told him that he would contact them. After three nights on the road, he and Farley were ready for a bath and a change to fresh clothes.

As soon as Purcell went up to the room, the clerk called a messenger over and told the youngster to go to the Stewart residence. The messenger was instructed tell them that Mr. Purcell, and a Mr. Farley had arrived.

When Purcell and Farley came downstairs, the clerk gave Purcell a handwritten message from Alisha with an invitation to dinner at six o'clock. They could come earlier if they wanted to. Purcell smiled to himself. She knew he would come as soon as he got cleaned up. He also wondered with amusement what Farley would do when he met Alisha's younger sister.

Morgan Stewart wondered what this Mr. Purcell would be like. He already knew that he was tall, handsome, smart, and wore a short, well-trimmed black beard. That was Alisha's description, anyway. According to Alisha, Purcell had attended preparatory school, but he lacked advanced training. It looked as if he would soon learn more about his oldest daughter's sweetheart.

Chapter 18

Morgan Stewart observed the two men as they approached the house on horseback. They turned into the drive beside the house, and proceeded on to the horse barn at the back of the property. They seemed to know where they were going, Stewart noticed. No doubt his daughter Alisha had furnished directions. Both were tall men. It was easy to recognize Stephen Purcell. He rode the big horse with the air of a man who knew what he was doing. There was no doubt he had Coldiron blood in him. This made Stewart feel a little uneasy. The Coldirons of Cross Keys had the reputation of being rough-and-tumble. All of them, as far as he knew, had moved west. The one named Granville had returned about fifteen years ago and married the widow Smith.

Alisha had said that Stephen Purcell was twenty-one years old. He looked older than that. In these times men aged fast. He could not have seen any more difficult times than Alisha. Maybe they would be a good match. Without a doubt, they were both tough, resilient personalities.

Alisha met them at the front door. She embraced them both and embarrassed Farley. She ushered them into the setting room and made the introductions. Alisha then excused herself to help her mother and sister in the kitchen.

"So you are Granville and Eppie's grandson?" asked Alisha's father.

"Grandnephew to be correct, sir," Purcell answered.

"I understand Granville was quite the adventurer."

"Yes, he was. He was a man of many talents. He could communicate in Spanish, French, and several Indian dialects. He led an amazing life. A life that was cut short by one of the murdering bands that operated under the excuse of war."

"Well, I am sure there were bands of outlaws on both sides," Stewart said.

"Yes sir, I agree, there were, but the men who murdered my aunt and uncle wore gray uniforms."

Stewart ignored the reply, saying, " I knew of the Coldirons. I guess I never met Granville. He raised and sold mules, so I have heard." He decided it would be best if he changed the conversation to another subject. "How about you, Mr. Farley? What do you work at?"

"I work for the American Telegraph," Farley said. "Shenandoah was my supervisor."

"I see. What did you do before you went to work for the telegraph company?"

"I was studying law, until the war interfered."

"You don't say. That is interesting. Who were you studying with?"

Purcell smiled to himself. He was off the hook for a little while at least. He wanted his new in-laws to like him, but Alisha was the only one that mattered. He would allow no excuses for what happened to Granville and Eppie...

Anna Stewart called them to supper.

Purcell was seated between Alisha and her mother. Farley and the sister were seated together opposite Alisha and Purcell. Mr. Stewart took his place at the head of the table. The conversation was light and pleasant.

The family was acquainted with Eppie and her first husband. Eppie had taught both girls in the lower grades. Anna asked if Purcell planned to return to Granville and Eppie's farm. He noted that he would, within the next few days. He added that he needed to find a place to stay closer to the property.

"I plan to go with him, on his first trip there," Alisha announced.

Her mother said, "Perhaps he would rather be alone."

"I can't think of anyone else in the world I would rather have with me," Purcell assured Alisha's mother.

"I am sure my grandparents can put us up at Port Republic," suggested Alisha.

"Alisha. Really!" Anna Stewart exclaimed.

"I am going with him, Mom. I am not leaving him to face that alone. If you are worrying about propriety, they have more than one guest room in that big house."

"Oh, my. She always was a headstrong person," Anna commented to the dinner guests.

Purcell smiled to the lady and said, "I love her dearly. She is her own person. And I would not have it any other way. She is the woman most men wish for, and very few ever find. I do not think we met by accident. I think divine guidance brought us together."

Morgan Stewart smiled, and said, "Mr. Purcell, you give a good argument. Have you ever considered studying law?"

"Please call me Stephen. My life has been filled, first with just surviving, and secondly with my telegraph work. I have had job offers from the telegraph, the railroad industry, and the Pinkerton Agency. Alisha and I will make a decision eventually. If she wants to continue nursing, that is what we will do. First there is the matter of Granville's livestock farm and land. To answer your question, I guess I could study law, but I doubt if I ever do."

"Alisha has told me of the circumstances of the property. I will be glad to help you with the research, should you wish. Also, there is Eppie's house in Port Republic. Land in the valley is normally valuable property. However, there is no money now. Northern speculators and grifters will offer only a fraction of the land's value. Eventually the economy will recover. But, it will be awhile," Stewart continued.

"I may need your help, and I appreciate the offer. Uncle Granville told me that he had deeded his property to me. He also owns property in the New Mexico Territory. I may need help in locating the paperwork on all of it. However, I am not aware of a house in Port Republic."

Anna Stewart entered the conversation, saying, "Eppie and her first husband, a Mr. Smith, had a small, but comfortable house in Port Republic. They both taught school here in Staunton, living here during the school term. They stayed at the house in Port Republic during the summer. According to my folks, Eppie kept it after she married Granville, and rented it out. The last renter left his family during the early years of the war and disappeared. The woman returned to her home in South Carolina."

She continued. "Granville had Moses Washington bring some help in and board it up. When the armies moved through, it was broken into and used as quarters for officers, by both sides. Each time they left, men from the community, including my father, would clean it out and replace the boards on the windows and doors. It is brick with a slate roof. That kept it from catching fire when all the burning was going on there. The buggy and horse shed behind it are in good shape. It has a small pasture. That is why the soldiers liked it. It is a very well-built house," she added.

Lawyer Stewart added to his wife's explanation. "There are no local property taxes and the Confederacy leveled no taxes on farmland until the very last. The war ended before they could collect. I can find no evidence that the Coldirons owed any money on any of their properties. Anna's parents said that it was local knowledge that Granville paid for both pieces of his land in Spanish silver when he returned from New Mexico Territory."

Stewart continued, "The tenant on the Cross Keys quarter section of farmland has paid Granville's share of last year's Confederate-imposed crop taxes so he could feel safe putting a crop in this year. Since most of the crops were destroyed, it won't amount to much. Mueller, the tenant, has continued to look after the Cross Keys property this last year, but he won't have any rent money. If it was left to me I would call it even. You will need to talk to him, and let him know what you intend to do. He has had his crops burned twice. He has been hit pretty hard. He has planted some crop on the land this year, but he is short on horse and man power."

Alisha moved quickly to explain. "Actually, I asked my father to check on the stock farm you lived on. He found public records on the other two pieces of real estate, also."

Stewart added, "Alisha said that you were wondering if Granville's bank account at Harrisburg had survived. I took the liberty of checking with the Bank of Harrisburg when I was over there last week. They told me that Granville still had an account there. It is a joint account, and that your signature is still on file. So you should have access to the account with identification. I reminded them that you were very much alive, and would soon become my son-in-law. That was all the information they would give me without a letter from you.

"Many banks have folded. I believe that one will survive. The rumor that your uncle buried his money, and that he did not trust banks, seems to be untrue. If I may ask, what did your uncle do in New Mexico Territory?"

"Father," Alisha scolded.

"It is okay," Purcell assured her. "To answer the question, you need to know that he went to the mountains to trap fur. He was trying to make money to start married life with his childhood sweetheart, Eppie. He didn't blow his money like most trappers. He took payment from the fur buyers in Spanish silver and some gold coin. After a year or so, he and his partner started back with their money in small bags. In the Kansas Territory they found themselves being stalked by Indians. During the Indian standoff, they buried their bags of money under a cactus plant.

"They were eventually captured by the Indians. The partner was killed outright. Granville was held and tortured, but he escaped back into the mountains after nearly dying in the Jornada. He was forced to spend another winter near Taos.

"Two years had went by before he was able to get back out on the plains, dig up the silver, and return. Eppie had been told he was dead. She had just recently married another, so he went back out west. Hurt, sick at heart, but unbeaten."

"That is a sad, heartbreaking story," Anna commented.

"There is more to it. Granville was a shrewd man. It did not take him long to figure out there was more money to be made in hauling and selling trade goods over the Santa Fe Trail, than in trapping fur. He used his silver to buy goods in St. Louis, Missouri, and shipped them up the the Missouri River to Fort Osage, and loaded them on wagons. Later he hauled trade goods out of Westport Landing, Missouri.

"Granville once told me about buying new double-barrel percussion lock shotguns for thirty-five dollars apiece in St. Louis, and selling them in Santa Fe for the equivalent six hundred dollars each. That part of the world had silver, but almost no manufactured goods. Over the years he made a small fortune. When Eppie's husband died in an accident, Granville came home. Eppie and Granville married, spent the rest of their years raising quality mules for the Valley's farms, and enjoying each others' company. They were getting up in years, but they still had some time left. That fateful day ended it for both."

Anna changed the subject saying, "My, my, here we are talking over a table full of dirty dishes. Gentlemen, why don't you retire to the sitting room and we will clear the table?"

"When do you intend to go to the home site?" Stewart asked Purcell after they'd settled on couches in the sitting room.

"Farley will leave tomorrow. Alicia wants to show me the church that we are to be married in, and the Jennings family wants us to have dinner with them. So, I imagine we will go to Port Republic the day after."

"Mr. Farley, where do... I guess he did not follow us over."

Purcell grinned, "I think he stayed to help Bea dry the dishes."

"Sometimes," Stewart said. "I think, I am beginning to get old. What about this fellow?"

"Mild-mannered, well educated, a gentleman, wants to learn as much about the world as he can. His polite manner masks his abilities. He is the kind of fellow you want watching your back. When trouble happens you can count on him holding up his end."

"I see. Well, I hope one wedding is all we will have this year."

Purcell saw Farley off on the early train. Farley told him that he had been invited back to the Stewart home.

Purcell hitched the team to the carriage, and went back to the Stewart residence. Alisha was waiting for him. "I thought you would never get here this morning. It is time for some hugging and kissing. I don't care what my mother says."

Purcell only had time to say, "I missed you, too."

Finally Alisha said, "I have several things planned today. First we will go by the church and meet with the parson. We will meet and pick up Aunt Clara, and return here to have dinner with the folks. Then we will go to the Jennings for supper. I know you are anxious to get to Port Republic and your uncle's farm. Earlier this week, I sent a letter by the circuit rider to my grandparents, telling them we would probably be there tomorrow."

The day went quickly. The church and parson were nice. Aunt Clara was even nicer, and a good conversationalist. After dinner, they visited Alisha's father's office. At the Jennings' home, Harvey made the introductions. The Jennings expressed their appreciation to Purcell for all he did to safeguard Harvey and get him back home.

Purcell related how Harvey's outgoing personality had won over his Union captors. He noted that Harvey was hard working, and soon found a place in the Brandy Station telegraph office. Purcell learned that Harvey was slated to be a cadet at the Virginia Military Academy as soon as it was rebuilt and opened.

It was a nice evening. Purcell knew that the next day he would start the last leg of his own journey home.

The next day, Purcell checked out of the hotel and picked up Alisha. She came out with a picnic basket for dinner. They retrieved her luggage and were soon on their way. The roads were rough, but Kathryn's carriage made the ride easier. He began to pass farms and homes that he recognized. Almost all the barns and storage bins had been burned.

They stopped to eat under a large shade tree and were soon back on the road. By mid-afternoon, they arrived in Port Republic. Purcell was sickened by the devastation he saw there. They stopped first at the house that belonged to Eppie. Purcell stared at it for a long time.

Finally he said, "I have passed this house in a buggy with both of them, and neither one said a thing about it belonging to her."

"She probably kept it because it was good rental income," Alisha suggested. "Let us look at it this way. Suppose you left, and someone with authority such as the military told me that you were dead. Finally I give in to the thought that you were gone, forever dead in a distant land. So, I marry a good, but uninteresting man. A few years later you show up very much alive. Both of us would be heartbroken... The house held memories that neither wanted to talk about."

"You are right. When I came to live with them, they were hugging and kissing on each other just as we do. I figured old people didn't do that, but they did. They were making up for lost time, I guess."

"Stephen, they were reassuring each other. It would have been a terrible ordeal for them, to have spent all those years apart. We must never let that happen to us... and Stephen, old people do that, too."

As they turned down the lane to Alisha's grandparent's home, Alisha said, "I want to warn you, my grandmother is liable to say anything, or ask any question. Usually, 'no' is a good answer. She is a delightful person. My grandfather is very polite and reserved. My mother has my grandfather's reserved nature."

The Littletons were waiting on the front porch. After introductions, Purcell took his carriage to the rear of the house and unhitched the team. He secured them in the partially burned shed barn.

In the house, the conversation was going non-stop. The grandfather explained, "Alisha and her grandmother have been apart for almost three years. They have a lot of catching up to do."

Alisha's grandmother turned and looked at Purcell. "My, you two will make beautiful children."

"If they take after Alisha or her grandmother, then we will indeed. I think I am seeing where Alisha's spunk, and most certainly her stunning good looks, come from."

"You didn't tell me he was a charmer, too," she smiled at Alisha.

The grandfather beamed his approval. The evening was off to a good start.

Purcell arose early and went out to grain the horses. He studied the damage to the Littleton's barn. Lumber, that would be one of the first things that this community would need. Someone needed to put the lumber mills back in operation.

In the case of Port Republic, replacing the burned flour and meal mills should be expedient. The task of rebuilding would be large. New grinding stones, if needed, must be ordered from Europe. He hoped the grinding stones of the burned turbines had been salvaged. They were turbine mills. If the wood structure around them burned just right, the turbine, drive shaft, and grinding stones may have fallen down into the water channel and escaped with minor damage...

Alisha was busy with breakfast. The grandparents were up and about. The conversation was pleasant, and reminded Purcell of Granville and Eppie in the morning. Alisha packed another picnic basket and made ready for the trip to Granville's farm. They crossed through the devastated town and struck River Road.

They passed through Lewiston Crossroads and drove by the Coaling. They proceeded around a turn, and left the River Road to follow a mountain road beside a run in the direction of Swift Run Gap. The road ended in a small valley in the shadow of the mountains.

Gentle slopes led each direction, and at the foot of the slopes in the meadow the charred remains of buildings were visible through the grass and weeds. The chicken house and the ice house remained. He recalled that Mose had said the raiders left the chicken house so they could catch the chickens. The ice house had been full of pond ice and wet sawdust. That's probably why it did not burn.

Purcell stopped the horses under the large oak. "It did not always look this way," he sighed. "See those pens and burned timbers up this run? Those were the breeding pens and shed barns for the Spanish Jacks and the mares. They were discreetly located away from the house. This farm provided hundreds of harness mules for the valley. Granville took his rent for the Cross Keys land in grain and hay. He bought more if he needed it."

Purcell drove on into the main farmstead, stopping the carriage at the front gate. He helped Alisha down and pulled the Henry from the carriage. "You might not want to walk through this mess. Granville used sheep to keep the grass and weeds down. The hands got the wool in exchange for shearing them. Uncle Granville never had to worry about getting the sheep sheared."

He walked over to the original grave site. Someone had smoothed out the disturbed ground and planted grass. "Mose would have done that," he thought to himself.

"Where did they bury the two raiders that Eppie and Granville killed?" Alisha asked.

"The raiders loaded the bodies across the horses and took them out of here. Mose said they buried them over in the churchyard. Mose and Bos Hartley kept track of what went on here for several days. I am sure they would have sent one of their field hands up in the timber, to watch below.

"Mose said the raiders came back a few days later and dug through the cooled-down ashes, looking for hidden hard money. All they found was a few silver dollars that had been in the house. I thought Eppie had some money hid in a cookie jar, or somewhere. Granville would tell her how much he needed and she would later give it to him out of her apron pocket. It was almost always in gold coins. Half Eagles, Eagles, and Double Eagles."

Purcell and Alisha made their way back to the carriage. He was reluctant to leave, and drove around behind the house ruins to Eppie's starter garden. There were some volunteer flowers growing there. Purcell intended to pick some for Eppie's grave in Port Republic.

"Some of the the last words Granville said to me were about this garden."

"What exactly, did he say about it?"

"Lets see. He said, 'Take care of Eppie's starter garden. It has considerable value.'" Suddenly the realization struck them both.

"Stephen! If there is anything here, this is where it is at!"

Slowly, Purcell got off the carriage. He reached in the back, and got McCorkle's gift shovel. He knocked the weeds down around the stone wall so Alisha could join him. She dismounted and stood beside him.

"Granville built this after they were married. I remember hearing him say that he hired a crew to construct the original stone wall across the back of the yard. But, he himself constructed this stone wall for Eppie's corner garden."

The flat stones were carefully lain, and sealed in with burnt lime mortar. The thick laid-up stone corner posts held the ends of cedar rails to keep the sheep out. "I have dug all over that little garden, planting and getting it ready for planting," Purcell mused aloud. "So it would be the corners, or along the fence. Eppie got the money for Granville by herself. He would not have asked her to do any digging." Purcell walked to the nearest post. The tops were slanted with an overhanging eve at the back to drain the water off.

Alisha watched as Purcell crawled through the rails and examined the stones under the eve of the roof stones. The two posts he could see looked alike. He pried and poked on the nearest post with the tip of the shovel blade. He thought one stone moved. He put his hand on it and tried to shake it. It would not come out but it was obvious that it was slightly loose. Somehow it was keyed in. He found that the header stone would slip up about an inch into the roof stone. He held it up with his left hand and pulled out on the large stone underneath. It opened out like a kitchen range oven door. It had been cleverly hinged and mortised in. In the hollow post he could see metal canisters sitting on some small dark metal bars. The dark metal bars would be tarnished silver.

"We must take this all out! Somebody could track us right to it." He looked around, hoping that no one was watching the place.

"First you need to see what it is. Let us take the metal boxes and set them on the carriage luggage gate," Alisha suggested.

They counted out over forty-thousand dollars in gold coin. "I know Granville sold mules, and stood Spanish Jacks here for ten years or more, for cash or gold coin. But, I know he did business with the bank in Harrisburg, too. He deposited the paper money and bank drafts. Two years ago, he had me go with him to the bank and sign the signature paper. He told the banker that he was getting up in years and if something happened to him, he wanted me to be able to do business.

"I am sure he brought the small silver bars from New Mexico Territory. One canister of coins are older, he could have brought them with him, too. I don't know what to do with it."

Finally, they decided to leave the silver bars and one can of coins hidden in the post. They would keep some for expenses and deposit the remainder in the bank at Harrisburg. Three canisters of five, ten, and twenty dollar gold pieces were left in the carriage. Purcell drove the rig all around the yard and over-grown lots just to disguise the tracks to the garden.

"The raiders thought my sack of potatoes was hidden booty. Rather than disclose that it was hidden, I think I will not tell anybody otherwise."

"Stephen you worry too much."

"I can't help it. Caution has became my nature."

"Is it alright if I go to the bank with you tomorrow? I lived and worked in Harrisonburg for a year. I know the banker and other people there."

"Sure, I figured on you going. We can keep one can and deposit two. That will give us some money in hand to work with until we decide what we are going to do. Alisha, we can build or buy us a house anywhere we want to."

"Where do you want to live?" Alisha asked.

"This is one time in my life I don't quite know what I want to do. I need to get some buildings back on the mule farm. If we choose to work, and live in town, we could consider Harrisonburg or Staunton. However, these rural communities are in dire need of grist mills and lumber mills. The people are good people that need help. They are going to need every man, and every dollar they can scrape up."

"That is what I thought you would say. Let us look over your aunt's house. The paperwork for it is in the bank. The banker told father more than father wanted to admit to you. We can clean and fix it up to start with. Two weeks from Saturday, we are going to need a place to live."

"We can get it cleaned up. But, we won't have any furniture. With all that has happened, the furniture must be shipped in."

"Stephen, I have been living in a church cloak room. You have been living in a granary. Grandmother said there is a kitchen stove, a table, and chairs in that house. All the furniture we are going to need to start with, is a bed."

The End

ABOUT THE AUTHOR

Walt Ryan was born in Cheyenne County, Kansas. The first home he can remember was a sod-walled house located on a rise south of the Republican River. He attended his first eight years of school in one room school houses on the high plains and in the Missouri Ozarks. Ryan grew up with an appreciation for the people of the western frontier, then and now. He enjoys writing about them in fact and fiction.

Ryan has lived and worked in the plains country and traveled the West. As a youth, he worked as a combiner on the wheat harvest circuit beginning on the Waggoner Ranch in Texas, and finishing the season on the Rosebud Indian Reservation in South Dakota. When Walt Ryan writes of horses and cattle, he does so with first hand knowledge. Ryan's many work experiences include mill hand, long haul truck driver, newsletter editor, photographer, writer, electrician, and over the years he worked through the ranks at several consumer cooperatives.

Ryan's work has been published in the Ozarks Mountaineer, Rural Missouri Back Page, The Iron Men Album Magazine, Rural Missouri Guest Column, and various midwest publications. In addition to writing books and posting on his blog, he enjoys collecting antique firearms and horse gear. Ryan currently lives with his wife Denny in Mid-Missouri.

www.SundownTrailBlog.com